EXTINCTION WARRIOR

One Girl's Round-the-World Quest to Find Her Parents and Save Endangereds

Susan B. Wile

*To Zoe,
The world needs YOU
thank you!
Susan B.*

Although all locations are real, this is a work of fiction. Names, characters and incidents are the product of the author's imagination. Any resemblance to actual persons, living or dead, or events is entirely coincidental.

Copyright © 2023 by Susan B. Wile

Cover art copyright © 2023 by Kristina Gehrmann

Copyright maps © 2023 by Rick Holland

ALL RIGHTS RESERVED.

Published in the U.S. by Turtle & Seed LLC.

No portion of this book may be reproduced or transmitted in any form or by any means, electronic or mechanical, including photocopying, recording, or by any information storage and retrieval system without written permission from the publisher or author, except as permitted by U.S. copyright law.

ISBN 979-8-9881076-5-1

Summary: In the year 2055, twelve-year-old Luki Sloan activates an android and masquerades as animal traffickers to find White Wolf, leader of the Red Dragon Gang in the hopes of finding her parents who go missing after hunting him down. After collecting a diverse assortment of endangered animals, they locate White Wolf and gain access to his superyacht where disaster strikes, and they confront a series of shocking discoveries.

EXTINCTION WARRIOR is printed on paper certified by the Forest Stewardship Council® (FSC®) that comes from responsibly managed forests that provide environmental, social and economic benefits.

EXTINCTION WARRIOR

Contents

Dedication	VIII
Epigraph	IX
Blurbs	X
1. Red Dragons on Saturday?	1
2. SOS Island Level Five	12
3. Aana, Taata, VR and Doughnuts	16
4. Blue Trance Micro Bolts	25
5. Droid Activation	32
6. A Plan to Masquerade	41
7. I Need You to Lie	49
8. Spiritcords and Mindsight	57
9. Slimendiggers, Nuwa and Uma	71
10. Antoadia and the Earwig	79
11. A Blonde Boar and Bison	88

12.	Vomit Shots for the Vulture	101
13.	Totipotent Cells and Ssanibot	113
14.	Termites and the African Wild Dog	117
15.	A Dehydrated Tortoise	128
16.	Pangolins and the Wrong Tattoo	138
17.	Phishing on the Road to Mandalay	147
18.	All We Have is Each Other	156
19.	Salesman on a Ship from an Octopus's Dream	161
20.	The Baby Needs Milk	172
21.	Was Ist Los?	182
22.	Neural Network Damage and a Werewolf?	190
23.	Down into the Dark	199
24.	A Jungle? A Cryolab? Mom and Dad?	204
25.	Endangered DNA and the Last Pangolins	210
26.	Flying Backwards in Time	217
27.	IMAGINE	223
28.	DISCUSSION QUESTIONS	225

| Afterword | 229 |
| About Author | 234 |

Acknowledgments

For all the extinction warriors.
Our precious planet needs you,
now more than ever.

"In wildness is the preservation of the world."

-Henry David Thoreau

Blurbs

"Original. Fun. Exotic. Action-packed. Educational. Inspiring. And Tuk is a great character." – Kate Klimo

1
Red Dragons on Saturday?

Virtual reality is the only way I'm free to escape the tundra and explore different worlds. In the worlds of *my* creation, I command the weather, control day and night, the seasons, the animals, the rivers, the mountains, the meadows. I can be away from the Arctic, the wind, the water, and this barren, boring, treeless place. Wales, Alaska—the westernmost place on the North American mainland is where I call home. It's frozen most of the year, almost always smells like snow, and the two months that everything thaws, it's nothing but a massive wet sponge. Okay, a lichen, berry-filled sponge, but a *sponge!*

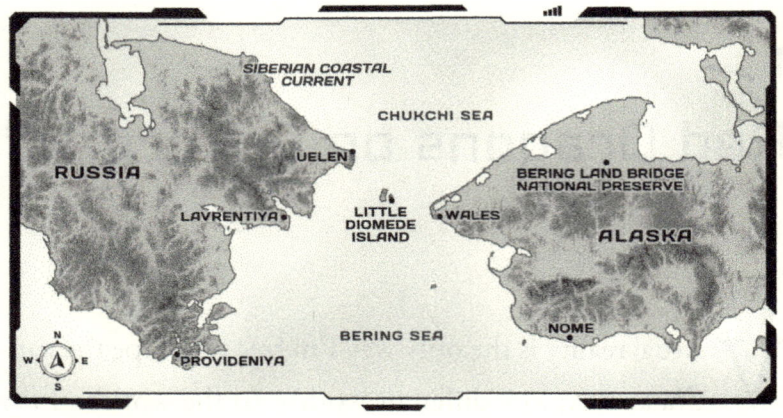

On the edge of my bed in my underwear and long sleeve t-shirt, I'm pushing my bionic foot through the leg of my haptic jumpsuit. With it, I can feel everything in the virtual game I co-create with my best friend, Korave, who lives in Russia. In the SOS Island adventure we started last weekend, we created a huge wild dog and released it on the savanna with miniature animals. Korave said I should be the one to talk to the elephant matriarch because I talk to animals with my mindsight in the real world. I can see what they're thinking in images they send me and feel what they're feeling and I let them know what I'm thinking by sending my pictures. Anyway, I've got to tell the elephant queen something that will let us progress to the next level, to a new ecosystem.

Migalik, Mig for short, is curled asleep on my bed. He's my pet arctic fox. His name means slush ice and his gray summer fur is coming in already, *super early*. I wouldn't have a single friend if it weren't for Mig. There's no one here my age. All the villagers are old, and if I didn't have Korave and VR, I might as well live on an exoplanet.

My parents crack the door open—Mom's petite and Dad's over six feet tall so his head sticks up above hers. They're peering at me in their uniforms. On a Saturday? Dad's lab day? Weird.

"Sweetie, we looked at drone video this morning, and the scant ice in the Strait melted earlier than ever." Dad frowns, shaking his head.

"Climate change." Mom nods.

Dad adds, "The big boil."

As if I didn't know. You'd think by 2055 we would have done everything possible to control climate change, what Dad calls the big boil, but we haven't because humans are basically greedy. And stupid.

"That means spring migration is earlier too." Mom's southern drawl comes through on 'migration.'

They're both scientist-detectives—agents for World Endangered Animal Police Protection—WEAPP for short. They patrol the Bering Sea and the Strait to monitor the thousands of belugas, bowheads and gray whales that swim north in the spring to feed in Arctic waters. They're all endangered, along with pinnipeds, and what's left of the birds that migrate here too.

"Red Dragons?" I ask, knowing the answer and my skin crawls with goosebumps, even though it's warm inside.

They nod, watching as I squeeze my real foot through the other pant leg, stand, shove my arms through the sleeves, and pull the zipper to my neck. The stretchy, skintight black suit almost makes me feel like a superhero. *Almost.*

"Hunting bow heads and belugas, no doubt." Mom sighs, her mouth drooping.

"And walrus," Dad adds.

"Hunting the endangereds that migrate through the Strait to the Arctic Ocean." Mom squints, her mouth pursed.

Flattening my braid for the helmet, I blurt, "I hate Red Dragons!"

"We hate the worst international trafficking gang, too," Dad sighs.

Red Dragons specialize in endangereds. They come in their monstrous boats as soon as the ice melts. There's nothing more dangerous than hunting them, especially during migrations, and it's why we live in the most desolate village, a hundred miles below the Arctic Circle, with just forty-eight Inupiaq neighbors.

"We'll meet our Russian WEAPP friends off Little Diomede and head north as a team into the Chukchi," Dad explains, then changes the subject to make me feel better. "Hey, thanks for helping load the android's mindfile yesterday. Let's fully activate him tomorrow to experience his humanness, huh?" He grins hard with a nod.

"Okay," I nod back, my breathing shallow.

Mom rubs my arm. "After your game, maybe you could work on your song?"

"'K." I nod but know I won't feel like it. I'll be too worried, and my mindsight will flash on them in the Strait.

They think my song will inspire kids and help end the extinction. That my song could save endangereds. I've always written poems and songs, and I draw too, the old-fashioned way, with pencils and markers. I was three when I made up my first song about Mig. I'm twelve, and the only way my song would make a difference would be for Nuwa, the number one world artist, to sing it. Nuwa would *have* to sing it.

I pull on my haptic gloves and snap the cuffs. "Dinner with Aana and Taata again?"

"You love her pickled sea squirts, Luki!" Mom grins, using the name I gave myself.

My real name is Wilhelmina, after Dad's mom. They called me Mina, but I liked Luki better. As a toddler, Aana called me her Qalukisaq, her butterfly. I only heard the Luki part, so I shortened it the way I shortened their names: Aanaruaq and Taataruaq became Aana and Taata. They're not my actual grandparents but might as well be. I never knew the bio ones who died before I was born. Aana and Taata live next door and were my parent's first friends. Growing up here I feel indigenous. Korave calls me his favorite pseudo-indigenous, trans-human hybrid.

"Taking *Barracuda* or *Anniqsuqti*?" I sit, give Mig a pet, and pull on my boots. Petting Mig makes me less nervous.

"The ASV," Dad confirms.

Autonomous Surface Vehicle, ASV for short. That's *Barracuda*, a boat, armored, like a tank. They take it when they want to catch criminals.

"I swear, you look like an extinction warrior in that jumpsuit, doesn't she, Ginnie?" Dad turns to Mom and smiles wide, exposing the gap between his front teeth.

"And one day, our amazing daughter will be," Mom says.

No way will I be a WEAPP agent! I'll design VR and fight the Sixth Extinction from a safe, warm, super comfortable studio. My games will help kids become more compassionate and change how they feel. They'll *want* to save the endangereds.

I smile at Mom and my mindsight flashes on pods of belugas—dozens of pale, shiny whales swimming under the surface in sparkly, Arctic water. With my parents in their ballistic helmets and bullet-proof vests, the water turns scarlet. "Be *super* careful!" I ask, my palms feel clammy.

"Always," they say in unison with a pout.

"Go to Aana's and Taata's after your game. We'll call this afternoon around four." Mom leans over to kiss my cheek. "I love you," she whispers and steps back, her curly shoulder-length hair tied back for work. She was a beauty queen and looks amazing no matter what she's got on, even her uniform. When she was a kid, she used to wear her hair in a braid, like mine. I'm taller than she is and even though my eyes are brown, like hers, I look like Dad with his dark blonde hair, pink cheeks and long, straight nose.

Dad wraps his arms around me and squeezes me to his chest. On my tiptoes, I squeeze back hard, and my heart jumps into my throat.

"I love you," I whisper, my cheek pressed against his neck, inhaling his beard oil, vetiver and cedar wood, like a grassy field on a sunny day. The lightscreen on the wall above my desk flashes a caribou face. Caribou grunts fill the room, Korave's ringtone. Caribou is his animal totem because that's what his father does—herd caribou. It's what

Korave means—*deer* because he was born into a family of deer herders.

"Back late tonight, paniga. See you in the morning." Dad uses Inupiaq for 'my daughter.'

"I'll make a yummy batch of waffles in the morning, and you'll tell us all about your VR adventure," Mom rushes her words, beaming her beauty queen smile.

"See you," I reply.

They leave, and I close the door and turn toward the lightscreen. "Answer Korave." The caribou head dissolves into Korave's face.

"Hey," I feel out of breath, and plop down in my chair.

"You don't look ready." He shakes his head. His black hair falls in his eyes and looks extra shiny. He's in his bedroom, in his jumpsuit, sitting at the metal table he uses to work on damaged droids. Droid body parts litter the floor and hang haphazardly on the wall behind him.

"Why you can't breathe?" he questions, with his thick Russian accent. He leans closer and stares at my face.

"My parents... I'm nervous.... they're heading out to catch Red Dragons."

"Nothing to fear. Korave always here!" He spreads his arms, like he wants to hug me.

I grin, my cheeks instantly warm. Korave's been my best friend ever since virtual school. He's smart, sensitive, kind and funny. Not stuck up like the rest of the kids, and I love his long hair, and the gap between his front teeth, like Dad's.

"New foot works excellent, da?" He smiles and wraps his hair behind his ear.

My turn to use Russian. "Da" means yes. Net, pronounced "nyet" means no. We go back and forth. Yes! No! Da! Net! Da! Da! Net! Net! Our game.

"Da! Fantastic, I actually feel my toes!"

"Feeling toes. *Very* useful. Da," he replies with a goofy smile.

"Da... but it's weird. My brain recognizes it's bionic and loaded with sensors, microprocessors, and super-propulsion, but it totally feels like me, like it's part of my body. It's even *better* than my real one. I'm almost glad I have an abnormality in one of my genes and was born with a limb deficiency. Da!"

"Like a real cyborg...net?" He smirks, "But truly...you are my favorite quasi-indigenous, trans-human!"

"Net! I'm just a little augmented is all. Not like those cyborg kids with intelli-chip implants. Net!" I shake my head with a fake frown.

"Da! Best for brain to learn original, primitive way. Plus, you don't want bald head from infection. Happens all the time."

Baldness from an intelli-chip implant infection? Disgusting. "Ew, net!"

He snickers, runs his fingers through his hair, and reaches for his helmet on the floor behind him. "You know what to tell mini pachyderm?" He asks with his eyebrows going way up. "Da?"

I nod. "I will when I'm with her... I think," and turn to look for my helmet.

"Let's go!" He pulls his helmet on. "Start SOS Island level five."

We have identical helmets—the latest model. It covers the entire head with built-in goggles and surround speakers, so we hear the entire virtual world. Plus, we *smell* everything with the scent activator, which makes all the environments hyper real!

"I am so ready to finish level five and move to level six!" He's excited, almost shouting.

"Wait, a nano... I can't find my helmet!"

But Korave isn't listening. He's already in the savanna.

I'm crawling on the floor, searching. Not under my desk, or closet floor.

"Where did it go, Mig?"

"Under the bed." He yawns, his voice like a purr in my mind's ear. My mindsight glimpses the picture he's sending—the helmet near my boot.

I crawl over, tilt my head sideways, and peer into the dimness. It's there. Must've rolled off because Mig pushed it, attracted by the aroma of popcorn molecules in the scent activator.

Before, when we stopped playing, Korave and I were next to a shrub that a leopard had sprayed to mark his territory. The urine smelled like *popcorn?!* It was so intense I had an instant craving and made a bowl as soon as I got out of my haptic suit.

I grab the helmet and dash to my VR space on the opposite side of the room to activate the padded screen that runs on a track from the floor to the ceiling. It's where I enter virtual worlds without crashing into my bed or desk.

"Activate VR screen," I tell the smartwall, and the screen rolls across the room, cutting it in half. Jamming my helmet on, I yelp, "SOS Island, level five!"

2
SOS Island Level Five

It's sunny in the savanna with distant storm clouds on the horizon. I drop to the ground beside Korave, who's on his stomach in the grass. We're close to a watering hole.

"There, she moves." He points.

"Yeah."

The miniature matriarch stands on the far side of the watering hole. Her huge ears almost touch the ground. She's about four feet tall, at the water's edge, guarding two baby elephants the size of goats rolling and playing in the mud. Impalas, the size of house cats drink nearby with zebras and giraffes, not much larger than me, waiting to drink.

"Here I go." I take a breath.

"She must *believe* you," Korave whispers. "Whatever you say, she must accept it, or we go nowhere."

I walk super slow, crunching the dry grass with each step. When I'm about eight feet from her, I stop, holding my breath. The little elephant queen flaps her ears, waiting. Waiting for me to tell her whatever it is that lets us move to level six. She has kind, brown eyes. Sincere. Intelligent. So *alive!* I listen like Taata taught me, opening my heart to what I feel, and finally whisper, "It's our fault."

Like a swarm of angry hornets, her low rumble envelops me in a cloud.

"When the colossal dog arrived," she declares, "we endured his endless chasing. The invader played at hunting and disturbed us with his sprinting that scattered everyone to the winds in a panic. He has learned to catch gazelle, but I am troubled for the gazelle, as I am for the lions, cheetahs, and leopards that prey upon them."

For fun, Korave and I made the African wild dog gigantic, way bigger than the rest of the animals in level five. He's disrupting the balance in this hot savanna.

She continues, swaying her head and trunk. "On his second day, he declared he was an apex predator, but had no family, no pack and was powerless to kill his usual prey, eating only what the lonely hunter could catch himself: mice, rabbits, hedgehogs – not his preferred diet." She stops, stares and flaps her ears, waiting.

I've got to tell her something else, but what? The baby elephants are curious, but fearful and crawl between the legs of the other adults gathering behind the matriarch. The herd watches and waits, getting agitated, ready to move on.

What else should I say? Is there something more I need to tell her? My eyes shift to the ground, to the queen's dusty feet. My heart pounds in my ears.

The dog is way too big for the miniature creatures in this environment. He's disturbing everything—like in the real world when invasive species take over and destroy the balance.

"I'm sorry." I shrug. "We're both sorry." It may only be a game but feels totally real. I'm tense, sweating all over. "I promise we'll make it better for everyone!"

Gradually she approaches and comes within inches of me. Her trunk starts at my feet and drifts back and forth up my legs, torso, shoulders, neck and head, exploring my scent, inhaling every inch of me. She exhales her warm, grassy breath on my face, lifts her tail and farts. I stifle a laugh and my eyes bug.

Korave snickers. We *must* be at the end of level five by now, but she's not responding. There must be another action, something we must do for her. But what? She's got to tell us how to advance.

Like air pinched from a balloon, she lifts her trunk and trumpets while wet, grassy clots of poop fall to the ground behind her.

"We accept your apology. Remove the dog, walk through my excrement, and move to level six."

I go limp, relieved, but ew!

All at once the air fills with a chorus of happy trumpeting. The elephant queen brushes my shoulder, and the herd trots off in a cloud of dust, wagging their tails.

"Excellent Luki!" Korave declares. "I would not think to apologize."

"We need to walk through her poop! Smell it? It's bad, and humongous!"

"Who cares?!" Korave jumps up and stomps through the mound triumphantly.

3
Aana, Taata, VR and Doughnuts

Strands of Aana's fine gray hair fly about her face. She stands with her back to the table at the stove in her kitchen, frying doughnuts and humming along with one of Nuwa's greatest hits drifting in the warm, greasy air from the lightscreen in the wall. Nuwa's so plastic, I swear she's a gynoid! Her phony techno-vibe oozes through any lightscreen—even their broken one! Aana's wearing her apron with pockets to protect her favorite baggy sweatshirt and sweatpants. Taata sits at the table across from me in his favorite plaid shirt, frayed at the cuffs.

The lightscreens in their house function terribly. Every three or four seconds, either Nuwa's face disappears, or the sound drops. They haven't upgraded in forever because they don't care. Dad's convinced voles in the walls have been chewing the fiber optics for years.

"Desert, huh? Never been to one and never will. Give me frozen any day." Taata shakes his head.

"Deserts are freezing cold, *at night*," I say.

"What'd you do?" Taata chews a piece of maktak, bowhead whale blubber he calls Eskimo chewing gum.

"Korave stepped on a massive spider hiding under the sand as soon as we entered level six."

Aana stops humming and turns toward us, holding tongs. "Spiders are helpful, but I don't like the creepy way they crawl with all those legs," and shakes her head with a frown.

Aana has the most expressive face. She can smile and laugh hard one minute, and in a nano, her eyes and mouth have all the sadness and suffering of the Inupiaq.

"Me neither, and this one had enormous jaws and tried to bite Korave's foot, but he kicked it in the mouth, and it crawled away. We got ten points for that."

"A good time." Taata chuckles, pushing his mustache off his lip with his finger.

"We could see the oasis with palm trees up ahead in the distance and kept walking, but my bionic foot caught something. I twisted around and my butt landed on a cactus."

"A cactus pricking your iqquuk? That would hurt!" Aana says.

"Yeah, and Korave was laughing really hard, and then out of nowhere, a two foot scorpion crawled from behind the cactus in attack mode with its tail curled, ready to sting. Korave stopped laughing in a hurry."

"Another reason I like Arctic." Taata grins, chewing hard, rubbing his chin stubble.

"With the cactus jabbing my butt, I reached out, grabbed the squirming scorpion and it ended up stinging itself. We got twenty points for that!" I smile widely.

"Sounds like fun, huh Aana?" Taata's eyes go wide and wrinkle his forehead even more.

Aana turns from the stove, biting her lip down into her tupiich, the tattooed lines on her chin. "Twenty points is positive," she nods, turns back to the stove and lifts a sizzling doughnut from the pot with her tongs.

"After that, we had to help a humongous beetle bury a ball of dung."

"Nothing more fun than getting rid of anak. We know all about that. Remember?" Taata smirks.

"Ohhh...when the village ran out of toilet paper!" Aana laughs. "The wind so bad that winter the supply plane couldn't land. No toilet paper for six whole weeks!" Aana laughs harder, and her eyes disappear into slits above her round cheeks.

"Ew.... disgusting!"

Aana sets the doughnuts between me and Taata.

I reach for a doughnut so hot I blow on it.

"The winter of....'42.... or '43?" Aana settles into the chair next to Taata with a cup of tea. Her sleeve pushed to her elbow reveals my favorite tattoo. On the inside of her arm, above her wrist is a circle with a dot inside. I asked her what it meant, and where she got it. She said it's an ancient symbol that represents nature's generative principle. A shaman gave it to her when she was nineteen, traveling in the lower forty-eight. I pretended to know what that meant, but didn't. One of these days I'll ask Yuka, the digital assistant on my miniQ.

Taata spits the gum out into his hand as big as a baseball glove. He grabs a doughnut. "I won't forget that winter, no matter how hard I try," he snorts, shaking his head and eats half the doughnut in one bite.

"So Luki...did you and Korave make it to the oasis?" Aana's eyes widen, and her forehead wrinkles up.

Another bite and Taata's doughnut disappears. He brushes the crumbs from his mustache and chin stubble, hiccups and pops the maktak back in his mouth.

After a bite of doughnut, I explain, "Eventually. We had to pass a group of vultures. Their heads were buried inside a putrid camel carcass that stank so bad!" I hold my nose. "We had to move like snails. We'd lose points if we scared even one of them off. It took half an hour to walk six feet!"

Taata nudges Aana with a grin. "This game gets better and better."

"We got to the oasis, found the well, and swam in a pool with gardenia flowers that smelled amazing!" I inhale and take another bite of doughnut. "We enlarged the pool and added miniature dusky dolphins that jumped, spun, twisted and leaped all over us. So fun! And at the very end of the game, Korave caught a horned viper and milked the venom while I got to hold the jar. We got fifty extra points for that!"

"Goodness." Aana takes a sip of tea. "What next?" She looks at Taata, smiling with her eyes.

"Level seven. The boring tundra," I take a bite, rolling my eyes. "We'll make it through that environment in no time."

"Since when are polar bears, musk ox, wolves, walrus, penguins, caribou, ptarmigans and all the endangereds here *boring?*" Taata's forehead wrinkles with surprise.

My lip curls. "Maybe boring isn't the right word." I squint with a shrug.

There's a cawing sound, and the lightscreen flashes a beluga whale—Dad's ringtone, a beluga vocalization.

"Answer Frank Sloan!" Taata's voice booms over the cawing.

The beluga dissolves into Dad's face in the pilot's seat on the *Barracuda's* bridge. Mom's next to him.

"How are things going?" Taata yells. He's going deaf and shouts whenever he talks to a lightscreen.

"Catch any Red Dragons?" I ask.

Dad grins. "As a matter of fact, we did," and turns to Mom, "didn't we, asik?" Asik is Inupiaq for 'dear one'.

We're all so used to the awful lightscreen and audio dropouts we understand what they're saying.

Mom nods. "From China. Two of them were about to kill a ribbon seal with their android. We turned them over to the Russians."

"You can always tell the XH5 droids. They're like Sumo wrestlers. Got terrific intel, too." Dad's eyes brighten.

"We know the endangereds they want," Mom nods.

"And they're not in the Strait." Dad shakes his head.

"Which ones?" I ask.

"They want endlings and the most critically endangered." Mom's mouth droops.

"And the functionally extinct," Dad nods.

"How come?" I ask. "I thought they wanted all endangereds."

"They do, but that's not where the big money is." Mom looks angry.

"Which ones do they want?" Aana looks worried.

"For starters...olins, cinereous vultures, radiated tortoises, Puerto Rican crested toads, African wild dogs, and Partula snails." Mom recites.

"Vultures?" Taata spits the maktak into his palm again and grabs another doughnut.

"Even vultures," Dad nods. "Folks believe that eating the bird wards off the plague. It's nonsense, but it's what they believe." It's so warm outside, Dad has his window cracked open.

"I hate Red Dragons!" I exclaim.

"Our Russian WEAPP friends have been tracking their leader, White Wolf. He's supposed to be heading this way on his superyacht." Dad reports. "Apparently he wants to watch the marine migration, or what's left of it in the Strait."

"Once we catch White Wolf, we destroy the gang," Mom grins.

A voice with a Russian accent crackles over the *Barracuda* loudspeaker. "*Yanbu* heading northwest at forty-three knots. Prepare for interception."

"Gotta go." Dad reaches for his ballistic helmet.

Mom puts her helmet on and waves. "See you for breakfast, asik," and adds, "Aana and Taata, come too!"

"See you." I wave.

Their faces in the lightscreen disappear, and Nuwa's reappears, warbling one of her greatest hits. I could care less.

"Time for a smoke." Aana heads into the living room to puff her pipe. I love her smoke, like a chocolate-caramel cloud.

"In this warm weather, how 'bout we practice igruraak? Always good to get stronger, throw faster, practice your aim." Taata nudges me.

When Taata was young he hunted birds with a bola he'd made himself. It was braided sinew and bones. I call it his Eskimo yoyo, but he only uses it for sport now. Taata taught me how to make one, so I made a couple with my favorite beach rocks and practice by myself, sometimes for hours. Usually Taata, Dad, and I go out back to throw from a distance to strike a pole stuck in the ground. Dad lets out a hoot when he swings over his head, but he swings too much and mostly misses. Taata says my aim is better than Dad's. When I strike the target from fifty feet Dad goes crazy, hooting like a cowboy at a rodeo. He pats me on the back with a big smile and comments on my excellent hand-eye coordination and strength. Taata always says the same thing. "You're a *natural*, Luki!"

"Sorry, Taata, but I don't feel like it."

"What about a game of Inukat?" Taata asks.

I'm bored with his game that I played almost every day after virtual school this winter. I know all the bones in his bag and can build the seal's tarsal bones to make a hind flipper in less than two minutes.

"Want me to beat you again?" I grin.

"Hmph," he grunts. "Don't think so. Grab the bag on the table." He points.

I reach for the bag of rough caribou leather and put it on the table between us.

He shoves the doughnuts out of the way.

"Got a different game. Traded with my buddy in Nome... let's see how well you know newborn tuttuk." He uses Inupiaq for 'caribou,' and dumps the bag in the middle of the table.

I stare at the pile of bones, but my mindsight flashes on my parents on the *Barracuda* bridge. A blue cloud surrounds the ASV and envelops the bow. It changes shape, forms into a ball, and hurtles through the crack in the driver's window. My parents flail, slapping, hitting, punching at the cloud. Closing my eyes, I take a breath. My eyes snap open. It's not a cloud. Whatever it is, it's alive—and attacking my parents.

4
Blue Trance Micro Bolts

I'm still in bed. My parents must've let me sleep in. My heart pounded with the roar of the wind all night. I couldn't stop thinking of that swarm of whatever and tried finding Mom and Dad with my mindsight. Hopeless. Did I even sleep an hour? Crack one eye and check my wrist miniQ. It's late. Eleven-thirty. Muffled voices in the kitchen sound like Aana and Taata.

I roll out of bed, shove my stump in my bionic foot, and head across the hall to the kitchen in my pajamas. Aana puffs her pipe nervously. She and Taata sit at the table in a haze of smoke.

"Where are they?" I ask.

"We don't know yet." Aana shakes her head.

"Talk to the commander?" I ask.

Taata shakes his head. "Commander Eetuk will call at twelve thirty."

My mouth droops. My teeth start to chatter uncontrollably. Suddenly I'm freezing.

Mig appears at my feet with the blue ball in his mouth. "Play!" He sends a picture of me throwing it.

"Not now, Mig." I lean over shivering and stroke his head.

Aana sets her pipe down. She gets up, wraps her arm around my shoulder, turns me around, and walks me to my bedroom.

"Shower, put on clean clothes and make your braid, I'll make breakfast. When the commander calls, we hear the *facts*."

I lean into her pillowy chest which envelopes me like a soft cradle and inhale her chocolaty caramel smell.

I try to eat Aana's pancakes, but it's like my stomach has a door that slammed shut. We're sitting at the table, waiting for the call. No one's talking except Mig, beside me on the floor, begging for a pancake.

"More!" He pleads on his hind legs, his front paws on my thigh, his chin on my lap.

I scratch between his ears, tear a pancake with my fingers, and drop a piece on the floor. If this were a normal day, Aana would scold, "Don't make fox your begging boy!" But she doesn't say anything.

The kitchen lightscreen announces, "Commander Eetuk," and reveals a brown, wrinkled face in a WEAPP cap.

"Answer!" I exclaim, and drop the rest of the pancake on the floor.

"Haluuġivsi," he delivers the Inupiaq greeting and takes off his cap. His kind eyes twinkle under the heavy folds of his eyelids.

Aana and Taata return the greeting.

"What happened? Where are they?" I ask breathlessly.

Commander Eetuk looks down at me, "Luki, I am very sorry. Your parents were attacked by a swarm of Blue Trance Micro Bolts."

"Drones!" I gasp. "Are they alive?" My eyes fill with tears.

Aana moves to me and takes my hand.

The commander continues. "Blue Trance Micro Bolts overpower targets by releasing chemical agents to anesthetize them."

Taata frowns. "Huh?"

"The capacity to kill is possible," the Commander pauses, "but their purpose is to induce unconsciousness."

"So, what about my parents?" My throat's dry, my palms cool and clammy.

He speaks with maddening calmness. "We are not certain they're alive."

Aana wraps both arms around me.

"The *Barracuda* was recovered by Russian WEAPPs who found it drifting in the Siberian coastal current in the Chukchi." He lowers his voice, not quite a whisper, "Russian arachnibots combing the beach for plastiglomerate found their helmets and vests washed up on the beach at Uelen."

"How long you keep looking?" Taata asks.

"We will continue the rescue operation today and tomorrow, but only until noon."

Taata nods, "Aarigaa." Inupiaq for 'good.'

"After that it becomes a recovery operation" Commander Eetuk pauses, sighing. "However, based on the size of the swarm, we suspect White Wolf might have wanted the Sloans dead."

No one speaks. I can't breathe. Feels like a walrus is sitting on my chest.

Aana finally asks, "How big was the swarm?"

The commander looks sad. "Blue Trance Micro Bolts are the tiniest military grade drone. The size of a large moose fly." He holds his thumb and index finger an inch apart. "when the *Barracuda* was recovered," he sucks breath between his teeth, and his words slow down, "the bridge contained over two thousand."

Aana gasps.

"...Surviving an attack that large... well, I just don't know," he shrugs, "...it's enough to anesthetize at least three polar bears." He shakes his head and closes his eyes. "I'm sorry." He nods, and puts his cap on. "I will call you with any news. Naanaakun," 'Goodbye.' And the lightscreen goes black.

I burst into tears. My bionic foot catches the chair and pulls it over as I race to my room, dive onto my bed, bury my head in the pillow, and cry myself to sleep.

It's dark outside when I wake and the wind has died down. Aana sits next to me on the bed. My burning eyes are swollen nearly shut. I probably look Inupiaq. I try to speak, but Aana shushes me with a chubby finger to my lips.

"Ataaaaaaaaa," she whispers, and shakes her head, "Before we know everything, we know nothing," and takes my hand. "We will learn all the facts and get through this *together*."

I nod as fresh tears come.

"Piqpavagin, Luki," she says, which means, 'I love you.' She reaches for a glass of water on my bedside table holding it toward me.

I sit up, take the glass and drink it down. "Quyanaq." I thank her. "Aana," I say, "what if they don't find them?"

She pushes the hair from my eyes. "Let's not play 'if' games. We wait to learn the facts."

"Okay," my stomach growls.

"Of course, you're hungry." Her eyes brighten and she stands. "Let's get you some food."

I follow her into the hall. "I'll check the farmoire for a ripe tomato."

Dad set up the farmoire last summer by dividing storage in half. It's full of lights, hoses and shelves with grow trays. By adjusting air temperature, carbon dioxide, humidity and light, we can grow just about anything. Dad got a seed vault too, with over five hundred different seeds. So far, we've grown lettuce, tomatoes, and cucumbers. I want to grow pineapple.

The lights blaze in the farmoire. I shield my eyes picking a tomato and some lettuce.

Aana scrambles murre eggs while I tear the lettuce leaves and slice the tomato. She and Taata sit in silence while I eat. Aana sips her Labrador tea and Taata sits like an inuksuk, a stone statue that marks the way out on the tundra. He's listening to his feelings. Tuning his awareness beyond his five senses. Tuning inside to distant worlds.

When I was six, sitting at the water's edge, or in his boat, Taata taught me to feel a walrus or seal coming. It might take all day staring at the water... feeling for the animal. It's like a rope of light that grows from my stomach and pulls the walrus or seal to me. No matter how long it takes, eventually it comes.

Sitting at the table, I imagine Taata's vision pierces the kitchen wall and goes down to the icy edge of the Strait, across the water to Russia and beyond to the Chuckchi Sea.

"Maybe turn Tuttuk on tonight? Huh Luki?" Taata suggests.

"Yeah, maybe." I reply, but don't care at all about activating the droid. I want to help *find* them! Staring at the Strait isn't going to bring them back. What can I do? *Nothing!* I've never felt more helpless.

5
Droid Activation

Dad named the droid Tuttuk, which means caribou. He said the droid would be essential to help save endangereds, that it had all the skills and expertise of a zoologist-veterinarian from the finest school, and that it would help us survive too, like caribou have helped indigenous people survive in the Arctic over ten thousand years.

"What would make you feel better?" Aana asks.

I know exactly what. "Calling Korave."

"Aa ii," Aana replies, "yes... of course, go now!" She shoos me from the table with both hands.

I glance at my miniQ. Eight o'clock. Korave lives less than two hundred miles away across the Strait, but on the other side of the International Dateline. That means he's twenty-one hours ahead. With a quick calculation...it's five o'clock tomorrow afternoon for him. By now he's finished his after school chore—reviewing drone footage of his family's caribou herd.

I'm petting Mig in my lap, at my desk in my room. From the waist up, Korave fills the lightscreen on the wall.

"Why *not* activate droid?" He's untangling a mass of wires erupting from the neck and head of an XH1 on his desk.

"I don't know...," I sigh, "I'm not sure I want to deal with a droid right now."

"He is newest model, da?"

I nod. "Da. XH7."

Korave stops messing with the wires and looks straight at me. "XH7? The most revolutionary humanoid *ever*, with a quantum computer for brain with holographic memory storing one hundred million terabytes of data." His eyes grow large. "Plus, XH7 memory bank has biochips filled with human DNA that performs seven quadrillion operations per second, with computational block chain processing. "And," he touches his head, "XH7 possesses synthetic consciousness."

Korave is an XH expert of every single model. He *loves* droids and wants his own droid servant one day he's going to call Spartacus.

I feel sad. Empty. Numb. "Yea, okay. He's got synthetic consciousness." I don't share his droid excitement. At all. Not now, and dig my fingers into Mig's shoulder fur.

Korave goes on. "This droid has the most advanced affective computing. Emotionally, XH7 is *the* most responsive droid ever, enhanced with ability to recognize and express all seven universal human emotions." He counts on his fingers. "Anger, contempt, disgust, enjoyment, fear, sadness and surprise. Droid has capacity to combine them, like real humans, to express a mix of emotions. Like for example, fear and disgust, or anger and contempt, or surprise and enjoyment. XH7 is incredible! Activate him! DA!"

"XH7's are beyond amazing. Da. I get it, but net." I sigh, stone-faced.

Mig jumps off my lap and onto the bed.

"Net?" Korave shakes his head, frustrated and scowls. "What I am trying to say... I want to be there, with *you*. You are my best, most perfect friend, but it's not possible. I cannot." He pauses, glancing at the droid on the table, "but your droid can be there. He can be your ally, and he... what is name again?"

"Tuttuk...I'll call him Tuk."

"So, Tuk can be your friend too. He can be there... with you." He points at me. "Plus, maybe he can help... da?"

I nod, but don't believe it. "Da, maybe."

A woman's voice shouts, "Korave!"

"Mama calls for dinner. Call me tomorrow. Da?" He smiles and his eyebrows scrunch.

"Da." I nod.

"Do svidaniya." He uses the Russian, 'Bye.'

The lightscreen goes black and I check the time on my miniQ. Almost nine thirty. I hear Aana and Taata talking softly in the kitchen.

Questioning my miniQ, I ask, "Yuka, what is generative principle?"

She begins. "Generative Principle is the driving force of caring, and how we generate our life experience. To generate is to create, and to create is to care. When you care about your thoughts, your words, your feelings and your actions, these become the will and determination that supports what you create. It is not enough to talk about the change we want in the world. We must care enough to change it. We achieve this by taking action to do our part, no matter how large or small."

I reach for a blue marker from my desk drawer. Rolling the sleeve of my left arm to my elbow, I draw a circle above my wrist inside my arm, halfway to my elbow with a dot inside it. It's not a perfect circle, but I like it. I have a tattoo that means I care, and I *will* take action. I just don't know what yet. Pulling my chair toward the bed, I reach out to pet Mig.

"I care about you... Mom, Dad... Aana, Taata, Korave, the villagers, VR.... and I want my parents alive, back home, and I want the Red Dragons to stop hunting endangereds!... and I want humans to end climate change for good, and the sixth extinction to end, but... I can't make *any* of that happen... what action do I need to take, Mig?!"

Mig's giving himself a thorough bath, licking his shoulders all the way down his back. He's not listening at all.

I stand and head to the door, whispering, "Overhead light off." The room goes dim, as I slip into the hall. The door to the kitchen and living room is cracked open. I glimpse Aana on the couch puffing her pipe, but she doesn't notice me. Taata snores in the chair nearby, his head on his shoulder. Turning to the right, I walk three steps to my parent's office. Open the door and close it, whispering the command, "Overhead light on," as the wind outside picks up, howling like wolves.

The room brightens, and Mig brushes my leg creeping toward the android.

Against the wall on the left, the wall facing the Strait sit two desks with a window in the middle. Tuttuk, lifeless, sits between the two desks, under the window in *my* chair, the one I've sat in a hundred thousand times. Mig sniffs the droids' legs.

The droid wears ultra-performance jeans, a short sleeved t-shirt, running shoes and no socks—the unofficial uniform for kids in school — virtual or real.

I take a breath, walk over and lift his shirt, dipping my finger down through folds of his smartskin membrane. It's like an extreme "innie" bellybutton that protects his activation key. I push down and start to count.

When I reach ten, he sits upright, puts his hands on his thighs, and opens his mouth for a full two seconds with a harmonizing tone that floats in my face. He's powered, but inanimate. To animate and make him fully "alive," I need to recite the numerical pass code Dad programmed him with; their wedding day, September 15, 2039.

Nervously, I lean to whisper in his ear, "9, 1, 5, 2, 0, 3, 9." He blinks three times and smiles.

"Thank you, Luki! Complete animation is a tremendous feeling!" He exclaims, his voice deep and gentle, sort of creamy. He rotates his head around the room, as his eyelids flutter under a mound of thick blonde hair that falls on his forehead.

To be like us, with our values, I helped Dad load the droid's mind-file data base with pictures, holograms and biographical information about our family, about Aana, Taata and the village, but we'd never completed the animation process.

Before, he was just a piece of equipment, a mannequin. Fully animated, he's so human, *so real*, it's unbelievable. Way, *way* beyond anything virtual! "Hi Tuk," I whisper.

"With your tendency to shorten names, shall you call me Tuk, and shall I be Tuttuk for your parents and the villagers?" He grins.

A wave of sorrow crashes over me. "Um, Mom, Dad," my chin quivers, "...are gone... missing... maybe dead." My eyes fill with tears, and I turn away dragging my arm across my nose and smash the tears with my palms. His cool hand touches my shoulder softly—his affective computing at work.

I turn back quickly, and his hand falls away.

"I need your help." I blurt.

"I am here, whatever you need," he nods, smiling wide, his straight teeth gleaming, his blue eyes sparkling. I'm stunned by how human he looks and *feels*, and peer down at Mig, who stretches and yawns.

"Good boy." I lean and scratch between his ears.

"I cannot tell you how fantastic it feels to breathe," Tuk inhales emphatically, expanding his chest, cooling his blockchain processor. "And hello, Migalik! You handsome arctic fox, white fox, polar fox, snow fox... phylum: cordata, clade: synapside, class: mammalia, order: carnivore, suborder: carniformia, family: canidae, species lagopus. I am not ignoring you." He reaches out to pet Mig who leaps away from him, toward me.

Tuk recites the scientific classifications like a song and shifts his attention back to me. "What happened to Frank and Virginia?"

I tell him everything the commander said. He looks at me intensely and listens without blinking or moving his face.

He frowns, and shakes his head. "Nothing in my data base has experienced a swarm of two thousand Blue Trance Micro Bolts. Is there anything else I should know?" he asks.

I speak over the lump in my throat. "My parents told us about the endangereds the Red Dragons really want."

"Tell me." He pulls his chair over and leans in close, our knees almost touching.

I say, "I didn't understand the first one, but Mom definitely said cinereous vultures... um, radiated tortoises, Puerto Rican crested toads, African wild dogs, and Partula snails—whatever they are."

"Quite a diverse assortment." He cocks his head staring into space.

My chest heaves and I stutter, "What can *we* do, Tuk?"

"We must undertake only one thing." He replies with a certainty that dissolves my helpless feeling and instantly I feel courageous.

He looks at the ceiling, his pupils dilating, and blinks as if his eyelashes are about to take off and fly away.

6
A Plan to Masquerade

"Tell me! *What?*" I'll do anything to help find my parents.

Tuk leans toward me and says, "We must find White Wolf. He knows where your parents are, and if we can, we must catch him."

"What?!" I scoff. "You have got to be kidding!"

"On the contrary. I am quite serious. This is not a topic I would jest about."

"Think about it, Tuk. Process that for longer than a nano—I'm twelve, and you're a droid! Did your biochips infused with DNA take *that* into account?"

"Of those factors, I am well aware."

"Finding White Wolf is one thing, but how do you expect us to catch him?" I'm sitting on the edge of Dad's chair.

"Simple..." he stares, expressionless, over my shoulder, "... we masquerade as Red Dragons."

"What?!" I sputter.

"Naturally we must obtain samples. Something to show him. We must have products to offer."

Sounds like he's talking about paint chips or wallpaper. "Samples? What sort of samples?"

"Endangereds, of course," he nods, "we must secure one of each; they want African wild dogs, a critically endangered species, and the Puerto Rican crested toad, along with the cinereous vulture, a radiated tortoise, and a few Partula snails. White Wolf will surely meet us when he knows we possess what he wants—his most desired endangereds."

I try to breathe deeply. "Sample endangereds? What you're saying is illegal... and what about the tattoo? Every gang member has one."

"I contain the design in my data base but will require your assistance to mark the tattoo's coordinates with the smartpen."

The pen? The pen! Where did Dad put it? I look around frantically.

"Each XH7 is equipped with one."

"You don't have the pen in your special pocket, do you?" I ask, worried Dad has it in *his* pocket.

Tuk stands, pats his pockets, and feels along his thigh.

He shakes his head and sits down. "The smartpen is a critical tool, and the sole means of modifying my smartskin. Perhaps it is here?" He pulls Mom's desk drawer out.

"Not there, I guarantee it."

"Correct. Nothing here but letters." He skims a couple. "The penmanship indicates these were written by Frank."

"Yeah. Dad's letters to Mom... he wrote her almost every day while he got his doctorate at Princeton."

I open Dad's desk drawer and breathe a sigh of relief. The pen's next to his fingernail clippers and a lock of my baby hair tied with a strand of ivalu, caribou sinew. "Got it!"

"Let me keep it." He opens his hand and I drop the pen in his palm. He leans forward to separate the seam of his pants, revealing a slim pocket at his thigh. Sliding the pen in, he squeezes the seam together, sealing it, then pulls his shirt off, and spreads his fingers around his arm to demonstrate. "The dragon wraps around the bicep onto my pectoral...here..."

His alabaster chest is rippled, smooth and hairless. The tattoo will be huge.

"...Once you generate the magnetic outline." He flexes his bicep.

He looks *so alive,* and his skin is almost iridescent.

"Even if we find White Wolf, I'm way too young to be in the gang. Why would I be with you? I mean, what *job* would I have?"

He pulls his shirt back on and sits facing me, pushing the hair off his forehead. "We pretend you are my younger sister, and...," pausing to stare at the floor, "... although not formally a gang member, you are my assistant."

Thoughts race... this will be super dangerous.... why should I believe a droid.... and why would I want to do this when I never wanted to be a WEAPP agent... Aana and Taata will never let me go... I'll have to lie... I hate lying.... what am I going to tell them.... will they believe me.... we'll go after Commander Eetuk calls... I should do this... what else can I do... need to call Korave... I could pass for fourteen, *maybe* fifteen....Tuk looks eighteen or nineteen... should we do this... can we actually catch White Wolf.... we might die trying... a wall of cages flares in my mindsight. My heart pounds.

"Why would White Wolf even believe us?" I ask.

"These criminals care about just one thing." He raises a finger.

I answer, "Endangereds!"

"No." He shakes his head firmly. "Money. Our youth is an advantage. In fact, our very adolescence makes us more believable."

I don't see how. "It does?"

He ignores me, his pupils dilating rapidly. Then he says, "Our itinerary is clear."

"It is?"

He stares at me like he's boring a hole into my forehead and says, "We need to collect the endangereds expeditiously. The most efficient route is to fly south to the montane rainforest of Tahiti for the snails; then east to Puerto Rico for the toad; across the Atlantic to the Caucasus for the vulture; south to the Serengeti for the wild dog; and east to Madagascar for the tortoise. Unless there is an unforeseen delay, that route should take five days, maximum. Your mindsight will help us locate the endangereds. White Wolf's headquarters are in Mandalay, in Myanmar. I believe chances are good we will locate him on his superyacht in nearby seas. This assumes the AEV is ours to pilot."

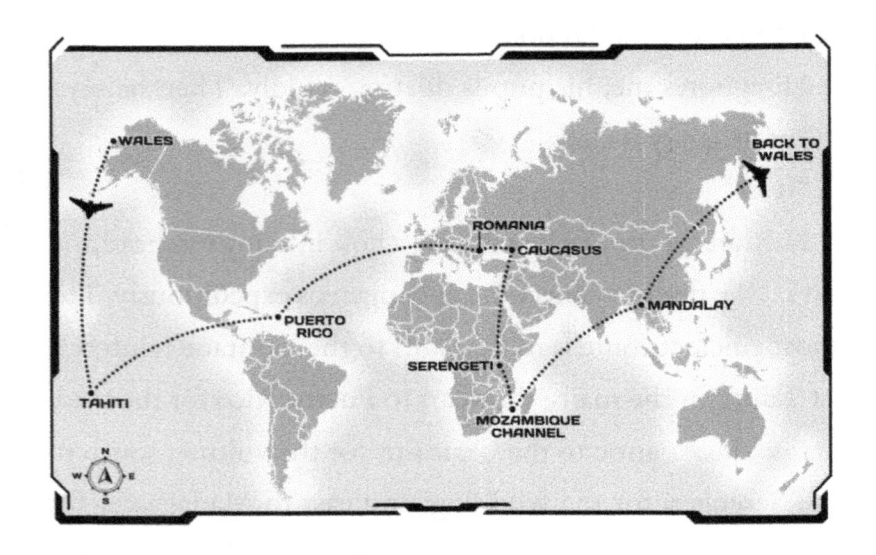

Tuk is convincing, but I'm not sure I should let a droid take control. Korave would probably say, *yes*. I'm thinking of Aana and Taata. I hate lying, but I'll have to. "Yeah..." I answer slowly and can't believe I'm going to do this...am I? *Really*? I never, EVER wanted to be a WEAPP agent. So, why am I going to do something insanely dangerous? Just because a droid talked me into it? That's so lame. But Tuk has extreme human skills and I can see spiritcords and communicate with animals with my mindsight. Still, that won't stop me from being killed. This is *terrifying*.

Noiselessly, the door swings wide. Aana pokes her head in, and I catch my breath, trying not to look guilty.

"Why, hello Tuttuk," she says.

"Hello Aana." Tuk nods.

"Happy to see you two are talking." She yawns. "It's three am. Taata and I go home to sleep in our bed." She nods toward her house. "See you in the morning, *paniga*," calling me 'my daughter.'

Now's my chance. I walk over, stuff my clammy hands in my pockets and take a big breath. "Tomorrow, I want to check the AEV's greenwall, um... see if the strawberries have ripened... and um... take Tuk for an aerial tour of the Preserve, maybe observe a bit of marine migration. Okay?"

"Oh, yes ... those strawberries! But what about Commander Eetuk?" Her forehead crinkles.

"I mean *after* that."

Aana shakes her head. "You never flew solo. Always had your Aanan or Taatan flying."

"Yeah, I know, Mom or Dad were always with me, but Tuk comes programmed to pilot. He's got certification built in. He can fly *any* AEV."

"From the Dragon Fly to the Thunderbird—I am certified to pilot every model." He puffs out his chest.

She sucks her breath through her teeth and raises a finger. "Back by dinner then, and no going higher than fifty thousand feet, or faster than seven hundred miles per hour."

"Quyanaq," I nod, 'thank you.'

She squints, momentarily suspicious. Then shrugs it off. "Unnualluataq," 'goodnight' she leans to rub noses and goes to join Taata.

7
I Need You to Lie

The next day, we're airborne, cruising along the Russian coast. Altitude just 70 feet above the water, slightly higher than the birds. I'm piloting from Mom's seat. Tuk's in Dad's copilot seat with his eyes glued to the water looking for whales. I spot a WEAPP boat, and my eyes burn with tears. Earlier, when Commander Eetuk called, he said WEAPP was doing everything they could to recover the bodies.

"Look, three o'clock," Tuk points. "A critically endangered Western North gray whale and her calf."

I pull myself together and add, "And straight ahead, six o'clock, another pod of belugas."

"According to my data base, likely extinct by 2123," Tuk states.

"Like so many cetaceans that have gone extinct in the last few years."

"Indeed," he lists them: "the North Atlantic right whale, the North Pacific right whale, the blue whale, the sei whale, the Atlantic humpback dolphin, the Amazon River dolphin, the South Asian River dolphin, the Indian Ocean humpback dolphin, the Irrawaddy dolphin, Hector's dolphin--"

"Gone. Forever!" I reply sadly.

"Nevertheless!" Tuk holds up a finger. "Depending on conditions over many eons, creatures evolve, new species appear... strange cetaceans may well roam the oceans in the distant future."

"Yeah, way after humans are extinct!" But I'm not thinking of endangereds or the sixth extinction now. I'm thinking about Mom and Dad. They might be gone forever, too.

Ice floe is almost gone. It's open water, nearly everywhere—basically, one humongous polynya with a scattering of birds riding the swells—mostly short-tailed albatross and spectacled eiders. A seal here and there. We're heading east, cruising around Little Diomede. A few birds are starting to nest on the island's eastern slopes.

I want a better look and reach for binoculars under the dashboard.

Tuk's head swoops back and forth, watching the birds scout nesting sites, and announces their names like a song, "there's a black-legged kittiwake... a parakeet auklet pair.... and one, two, three, four crested auklets.... and last, a least auklet."

"You're able to identify them from that far away?!"

"My optics magnify over 200 diopters."

Whatever that means, I guess he'll never need binoculars.

"I would like my visual perception system to witness six point seven million birds migrating to these waters, as they did a century ago."

"If you mean your eyes and watching that many birds? Me too."

We've spotted several beluga pods, and a family of bowheads—four of them swimming together, with two swimming behind. Following the Russian shoreline, we notice a few pinnipeds—the bearded, ringed, ribbon and spotted seals massed along the melting ice, clinging to the coast.

"Are you ready?" Tuk asks.

We're cruising further north above the Chuckchi Sea.

"For what?" I frown.

"To change course and head south."

My heart skips a beat. "I need to call Korave, and Aana. Wait, what time is it?"

"According to my internal chronograph, it is precisely two minutes and thirty nine seconds past three o'clock."

"That means it's..." I add twenty one hours ".... two minutes after twelve tomorrow. Korave's eating lunch."

"An ideal time to call." Tuk says.

I take a deep breath. "Tootega, call Korave."

Tootega is the ship's avatar. She controls all the systems and comes to life on the dashboard screen. With her brown hair and eyes, she looks so much like Mom, she could be her sister. It's why Dad chose her.

"Calling Korave Vasiliev," she states. In seconds, her face dissolves. Korave appears at his bedroom table with a half-eaten sandwich, a glass of water, and a droid hand with a tangled mass of wires hanging from its wrist.

Wearing his traditional Chuckchi caribou coverall, Korave shouts, "Luki!" with a mouth full and waves the droid hand.

"Hey," I wave back feebly, "I need to tell you something, and... I've got a request."

He swallows, lowers his voice, and suddenly looks sad. "Bad parents news?"

I swallow hard. "Disappeared. Presumed dead. Tuk and I are...on our way....to...."

"I'm so sorry...." he pauses, "but happy you activate droid," he says with a timid grin. "Amazing, da?"

"Da.... yeah, well.... I can't believe I'm doing this. It's like a dream.... maybe more like a nightmare.... but.... we're leaving... to find the leader of the Red Dragons... maybe catch him, or at least try."

Korave's eyes go wide, looks like he's going to choke and exclaims, "Net!" Coughing, he reaches for the water, and takes a sip. "XH7 more persuasive than any XH ever."

Tuk leans over my shoulder with a smile, "I take that as a compliment."

Korave grabs the droid hand and gives three thumbs up with his two.

I lean into the screen and whisper, "I'm petrified!"

Korave squints with a sweet-sad expression and leans in, like he's seeing into my heart. His face fills the screen. "Remember Death Trail game? You lead me through rain, fog and smoke. You did not fall off mountain path into snake infested jungle, or step on fat cracks in road with flames shooting out. Net. It was me who lost game for us." He nods.

I nod slowly.

"Remember Cave of Ten Million Bats?" Korave asks.

I keep nodding.

"It was me who slipped in guano." He thumps his chest with the droid hand. "I fall into nest of a thousand scorpions. Another great game I lost for us... also Labyrinth of the Underworld..." He points at me. "You found secret passageway out while I must crawl on hands and knees for hours in tunnels with rotten bodies hanging from walls that smelled terrible, their slimy flesh falling in my face! *Horrible!!* I bruise my knees and palms crawling all day." He holds up his hands. "But that one, I finally did win for us."

"But none of that was *real!*" I practically shout.

"Da. But you are smart and brave, Luki Sloan. Endangereds *need* you."

I shudder, nodding, and purse my lips. "And I need you to lie."

"Da! Of course!"

"Since it's spring break, I'm going to tell Aana you invited us for a visit... um, because you feel terrible about everything, and to cheer me up... that you want to show me your family's herd, um and.... that you want to meet Tuk. I'll tell her.... we're staying the whole week."

"It's true, I feel terrible, and I will say any lie for you, but if she calls, and you are not here, what should I say then?"

He's right. Of course, Aana will call. "Send me images of you and your parents, your house, your herd. I'll add me and Tuk digitally and send her composites. It'll look like we're together."

"But will she not want to talk to Mama or Papa? To hear invitation? Da?"

"Da. I'll tell her we'll arrive by six for dinner, but she should call at five thirty, before we get there."

"Da, okay!"

"But you've got to be in your room, ready to answer the call, and you *must* use the filter of your father's face to talk!"

"Da, okay." Korave nods hard.

I lower my voice. "You must sound like him. Make your voice go low."

He clears his throat. "This I achieve, no problem" he says in a deep baritone.

"Aana's smartwalls are so damaged she'll never know it's you."

"Sharp doughnut," Korave taps his temple with a smile, nodding.

"Um... the expression is smart cookie." I sigh with a grin.

"Call me, da? If something extra you need, I do it, *whatever!* No hesitation!"

"Da. Okay... thanks, Korave." I smile nervously.

"Do svidaniya," he says, waving the droid hand goodbye. "Also super udachi."

"What?" I frown.

"Good luck!" He replies with the droid thumb up.

The lightscreen goes black. I try to breathe evenly as I stare out the window encasing us in our bubble.

"Your friend Korave is kind." Tuk nods, his eyes twinkling. "He cares about you."

"He's my best *human* friend." I say, as a wall of white cages and a twisted mass of glowing spiritcords flare in my mindsight. I take a breath and swallow hard, dreading the call to Aana and dreading what I'm really about to do.

8
Spiritcords and Mindsight

"I like Korave. You *should* spend time with your friend." Aana pauses puffing on her pipe and adds, "Do whatever you need, paniga," calling me 'daughter.'

I feel terrible about lying, but glad she believes me.

"See you," I say weakly. Taata sits behind her at the table, expressionless, like an inuksuk. He says nothing, staring through the smartwall and the lightscreen, down through the village, to the edge of the water, and out across the Strait... right into my lying heart.

We've been flying at 65,000 feet, cruising silently above the Pacific for eight hours, at the edge of the ozone, the upper edge of the troposphere, crossing the equator in black, velvety night.

Tuk breaks the silence. "We are above the Southern Pacific Ocean, home to the Great Pacific Garbage patch, and the islands of Melanesia, Micronesia, and..." adds with a chuckle, "if I had amnesia, I would forget Polynesia!"

"It's physically impossible for you to forget, and even if droids could, you wouldn't—because Polynesia happens to be our destination." I frown.

"I am merely enjoying a bit of word play." He lays an icy hand on my shoulder.

"Guess I'm not in the mood," I grumble.

It feels like the lie spread through my body, like an infection. I'm glad to be distracted watching the compass, the altimeter, the airspeed indicator, the artificial horizon, the windscreen.

I learned about the ship and its Super Quantum Operating System, the SQOS before I could even read or write. It's a No Boom, Whisper Quiet, Supersonic, hydrogen-powered All Elements Vehicle—the Falcon model, with adjustable engines that rotate. It can take off and land like a helicopter, cruises like a boat, can submerge up to a mile, and has two levels. It's white, so Red Dragons don't know it belongs to WEAPP. My parents modified it to transport endangereds, with four faunal chambers downstairs, plus storage for the drones, spools for the printer, SSsanibot, tools and stuff. It even has a minuscule lab next to storage with a desktop cricket hive to breed house crickets for protein bars.

Stairs spiral at the end of the hall in the back, the aft. Upstairs, my cabin is on the right, like a jumbo pod with my bunk and Mig's cubby hole underneath. The head, or bathroom is in between my cabin and my parents'. I trained Mig to pee and poop in the shower, which makes cleanup super easy. The galley with the 3-D printer and greenwall, where we grow strawberries and lettuce is next to my parent's room, alongside the cockpit. Mom and Dad use the AEV to rescue and relocate endangereds. What they *used* to use. They named it *Anniqsuqti*—Inupiaq for savior.

I never made it up to my cabin and fell asleep in the pilot's seat with Mig curled in my lap.

Tuk startles me awake. "We must activate the QSC before descending into the troposphere."

"Descending? Already?" I ask.

"To conceal our presence." Tuk studies a map in the lightscreen, darkened for night flying, his face glows.

I rub my eyes. "Definitely."

"Besides breaking the air traffic laws of every country we fly over and into, starting tomorrow, we traffic endangereds."

I gulp and nod, stroking Mig's back. "Tootega, activate the Quantum Stealth Cloak."

Her face comes to life in the dim dashboard lightscreen. "Activating QSC," she says.

Tuk leans into me. "For the duration of this mission, best to leave the QSC on permanently. One less thing to remember activating after the ship has been in sleep mode."

"Good idea."

Like droids, smartwalls, mini and maxiQ's, the ship's avatar is always listening. "I know you heard that, Tootega. Confirm, audio only."

"Confirming permanent activation of QSC until notified." She answers without reappearing.

Tuk blinks. "My internal chronograph indicates three minutes past midnight. Since the ideal period to catch mollusks is during daylight, I recommend we land on the water north of Bora Bora, here," his says, his finger lights up as it points to the lightscreen, "in the protected, uninhabited lagoon at Tupai. I shall discern the optimum area of Tahiti's cloud forest for locating our tiny, sliming gastropods."

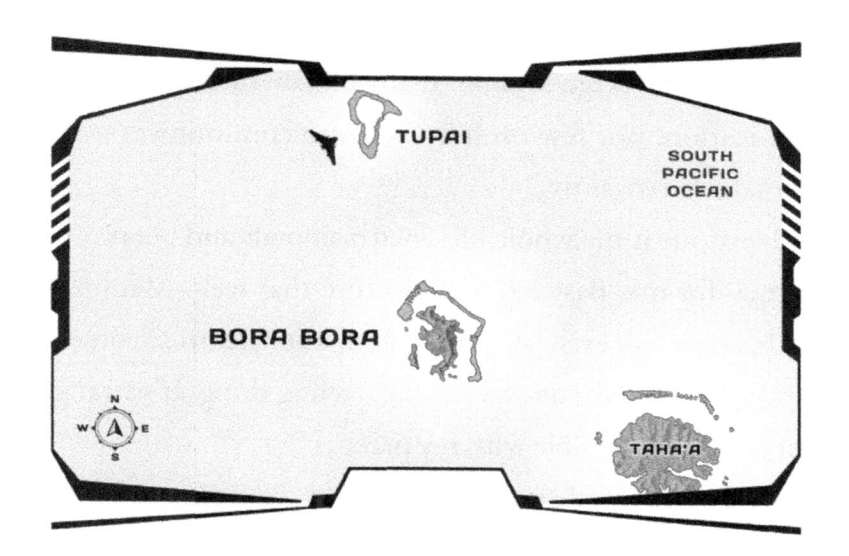

"You don't need maps, if that's what you mean. Once I know what they look like, I can focus my mindsight to detect their spiritcords. It should be easy closer to Tahiti. They'll lead me... I mean us."

"Of course, your mindsight! Can you describe your technique? How does it work to communicate with animals?" Tuk stares at me hard.

I hesitate. "Your data base includes thought transference, clairvoyance, ESP, mind reading, whatever you want to call it. My mindsight lets us exchange pictures—me to them or them to me—with our minds, our consciousness....it's how I understand them and they understand me. With pictures."

"Give me a nano," he blinks three times, and looks at the ceiling. "My storage contains many files on interspecies communication, but few on humans who communicate with animals clairvoyantly."

"I've done it my whole life—with animals and people. It's normal for me. Basically any creature that feels. Mammals, birds, some fish even. Anything with a spiritcord.... come to think of it, just about every living, feeling thing. It's strange, but almost impossible with my parents."

"And what exactly is a spiritcord?" He squints.

"They're like strands of living, pulsing light. They can be thin or thick, depending on the animal's health. If it's sick or wounded, they're dull and thin as a thread."

"What a marvelous a talent!" He exclaims and rubs my shoulder. "But a pity your ability does not include androids," he adds.

I glance at the course deviation indicator and change the subject. "We're one hundred miles from Bora Bora.

"That means Tupai is eighty-three point three miles away."

"I'll start the descent. We'll be there in minutes. Tootega reduce air speed and flight path ten degrees."

Just then, a spiritcord, a hair's width, appears in my mindsight.

We're hovering at 2,000 feet on the eastern side of jagged Tahitian mountains. The spiritcord led us to this one spot in the jungle.

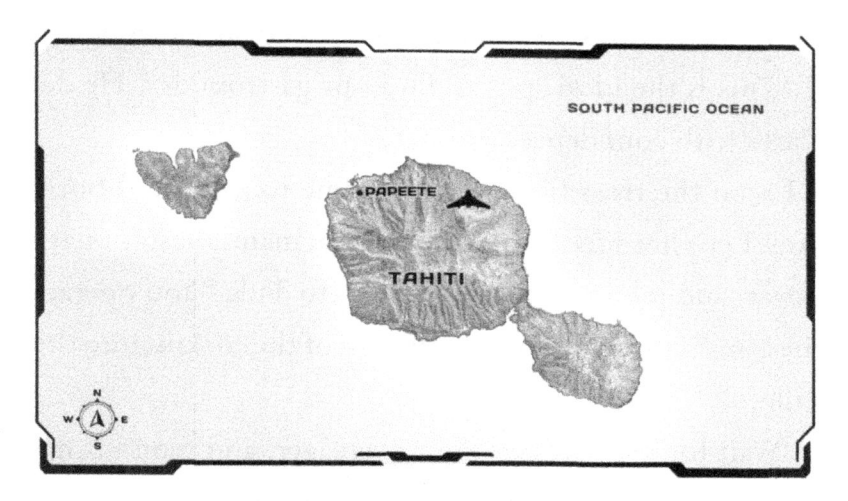

Tuk leans toward me. "Reduce altitude to one thousand feet and scan the mountain slopes for groves of banana trees. Partulas like the underside of their leaves."

"Okay," I sigh. It bothers me that he's so bossy but then I remember that Korave said droids always want to control.

"What does a banana tree even look like?" I ask.

"Fe'i bananas, typical for Polynesia, grow in bunches upward toward the sky," he sticks his fingers above his head, like antlers. "It should be easy to spot them."

With his robust data base, Tuk knows everything.

Cruising super slow, I bring us down to nine hundred feet. We're inches above the treetops.

"There! An enormous bunch." Tuk points, excited, "Three o'clock."

Shifting to hover mode, I maneuver close to the banana trees. Their leaves are oblong, and at least six feet long.

"This is the ideal spot to find our gastropods." He declares with confidence.

I scan the trees beneath us. "Time to use the robotic arm. Let's head to the galley. Tootega, maintain stationary hover, and release arm one." I turn to Tuk. "You operate the arm." I unbuckle, squeezing out of the cockpit into the galley.

"Wait for me!" he exclaims, overeager, and reminds me of Mig as a kit, who followed me everywhere.

We're in the galley at the folding table. I'm eating strawberries, just picked from the greenwall behind me. Tuk wears the gray, wireless glove on his right hand. Going up to his elbows, it's studded with hundreds of sensors. When he moves his hand and arm, the robotic arm outside duplicates his movement. The ship is equipped with six arms that release from the underside of the fuselage: two fore, two aft, and two in the middle.

Remotely, Tuk turns a banana leaf over, searching for snails, and out of nowhere, a blanket of fog rolls in. We can't see anything now.

"The very reason for the name *cloud forest*, and not at all helpful at the moment," he mutters.

Sensing my impatience, Mig appears at my feet with the ball in his mouth.

"Play!" He barks.

I grab it and toss it down the hall. Through the open door of my parents' room, I catch a glimpse through the porthole of brown blobs stuck to the wing. Strange conical coconuts. The wingtip must've picked them up in a cluster of leaves. Three of them are moving? They're ALIVE?

Turning, I point them out to Tuk. "What are those?!"

Tuk's leaning on the table, his gloved arm outstretched, like he's sewing invisible fabric. He answers without looking. "What are the those to which you refer?" He's staring through the mist at the mechanical fingers gripping the leaf. Even with his droid perception system, there's no way he sees anything out there!

Mig's in the hall, the ball in his mouth, waiting to play. Ignoring him, I step into my parents' room for a closer look.

I'm stunned at the sight of the blobs sliming up the wing. "They're the most humongous snails ever!"

"Lissachatina fulica." Tuk states, still without looking. "Giant African snails. One of the world's most invasive species!"

"I never knew snails could grow to the size of a baseball glove!"

"Yes, indeed. They were introduced to these islands as a food source during World War II. Unfortunately, any number of them escaped and reproduced prodigiously."

I'm horrified and fascinated. "And they're sliming this way!" I exclaim, heading into the hall.

Mig's got the ball in his mouth.

"Play!" Mig barks again.

"Not now!" I step into the galley.

Tuk has turned onto his back on the table. His head dangles off the side, scanning the leaves. As if plucking a harp, he turns his wrist, pinching thumb and index finger, turning the leaves over, one by one, scrutinizing every inch of leaf with his droid vision.

He looks uncomfortable and ridiculous. "You can't possibly inspect better in that position. Can you?"

"My comfort at the moment happens to be far less important than finding Partulas." He continues plucking the strings of his invisible harp.

"Too bad the giant African snails aren't endangered, or we could just grab them."

"The giant African snails are extremely invasive and lay up to one thousand eggs per year."

"The total opposite of endangered."

"Plus, they eat almost anything."

"Like what?"

He lifts his head to face me. "Everything from cardboard to sand, miniature stones, bones from carcasses, even concrete. Also, dead mice, birds and cannibalistically, other snails."

"Cannibals? That's disgusting!"

He continues to work. "They are partly the reason why so many Partula snails have gone extinct. But it was the introduction of the carnivorous Florida rosy wolf snails to combat the giant African snails that backfired. The wolf snails preferred the Partulas and devoured dozens of the species in a matter of decades. One disastrous intervention led to an even more disastrous intervention."

I step into the hall to check the parental porthole again. One snail has nearly reached the fuselage.

"We've got to intervene in a hurry and toss them back into the treetops before the monsters slime their way here and goo up the whole window. Tootega activate arm two!" I command.

"Confirming arm two activation," she replies.

"Hurry, Tuk." I nudge his shoulder. "Come on!"

He slides off the table leaving the mechanical arm dangling in the banana leaves.

With his gloved arm stretched out before him, he joins me in my parents' room.

The one snail has nearly reached the fuselage.

I urge Tuk, "Grab it! Toss it! Get rid of it!"

Tuk reaches out, his fingers curling around space. He makes a loose fist as the mechanical fingers wrap around the snail's shell. He grips hard, too hard. The shell cracks. Snail slime explodes and oozes through the mechanical fingers. Pearly snail eggs splatter across the wing, dotting the other snails, like sprinkles on ice cream.

"Ew!"

"I did as you directed. I grabbed the closest one and got rid of it." Tuk says.

"Geez Tuk, way too hard! You need to be sensitive." I reach my hand out. "My turn. Glove please."

Tuk rolls the glove down his arm, pulls the fingers off one by one, and drops it in my outstretched hands.

Reaching my fingers inside the hand, I pull the glove up around my wrist and wrap it tight, cinching it above the elbow. It's too big but doesn't matter. First, I practice flexing and grasping. Then I reach toward a snail and wrap my hand around the shell. Sensing its pressure on my fingers, I pull. There's resistance. Its sticky suction holds tight. I need to peel it, not pull it. I start at the front, firmly lifting, peeling the snail away to detach it from the wing, then spread my fingers and release it into the canopy. Repeat for the next snail. One by one, I remove the sticky suckers.

"You are a natural, Luki," Tuk says. "Impressive technique."

"I owe it all to VR." I reply when a flash of the thinnest spiritcords appear in my mindsight. They glow from the tips of the robotic fingers, like wisps of Aana's fine gray hair.

"Let's head to the galley," I say. "I'm pretty sure we've got Partulas there. Tootega, activate arm one, and release the galley hatch."

And Mig? Disappeared. Probably sulking in my cabin.

Drops of water vapor and snail eggs cover the galley window. The mechanical arm hangs invisible in the mist. Moving my gloved arm toward my face, the robotic arm appears in the window.

"There! On the fingers!" Tuk declares. "Five Partulas, sliming their diminutive gastropod feet on the index and pinky fingers!"

"Behind you, under the greenwall, in the cupboard, you'll find a vivarium," I command. Who's the boss now?

Bending the arm around, I push the mechanical hand through the hatch under the window. Tuk scrapes the snails off the fingers with a spoon and deposits them in the vivarium on the table.

"As detritivores, they require banana leaves for sustenance, which rot nicely," Tuk says.

"This fog's so dense, I'm blind. With your droid vision, that'll be your job. Hop to it."

9
Slimendiggers, Nuwa and Uma

While we hovered collecting banana leaves, the wind kicked up and blew away the fog. Tootega announced a tropical storm developing. Exactly what we don't need. We could see the leaves clearly, but no way could Tuk hold his arm steady. Like an elephant trunk, the robotic arm thrashed up, down, and sideways. It took hours to rip off enough leaves for the Partulas.

As soon as he finished, I take us to five thousand feet. The ship hovers on autopilot while we head to the galley. With a few heavy-duty suction cups, we secure the vivarium to the window.

"Super suction works well," Tuk nods, satisfied with his placement.

"Plus, the vivarium walls are electrochromic." I touch the bottom corner and the glass darkens instantly. It's darker outside, too, and raining hard.

"Excellent. We do not want the sun to cook our escargots." Tuk winks.

The inch-long mollusks slime up, down and around the leaves. In my mind's ear I hear high-pitched singing, "Our slime is prime!"

What does that even mean? A nano later, there's a chorus, "Slimendiggers." Coming from the snails?

"Ever heard of a Slimendigger?" I ask.

"Gastropods? Slimendiggers? How very appropriate!"

Around us, the ship starts to shake.

"Tropical cyclone Uma continues to gain strength. Expect extreme turbulence." Tootega announces over the intercom.

I grab the edge of the table with both hands. "Hold on, Tuk!"

The ship bumps hard—up and down, left and right.

We jerk and drop for one... two... three... four... five seconds. I don't need clairvoyance to feel Mig's terror as we abruptly lose altitude and the ship rocks and shudders harder.

"Let's get out of here!" I bolt down the hall to my cabin where Mig crouches in terror. Dad modified one of the storage drawers underneath my bed to make it the safest spot for him during takeoffs, landings, and turbulence.

"Good boy." I stroke between his ears, unlatching the cubby door.

He slinks in fast. I shut it, then race to the cockpit, jam my butt in the pilot's seat, and buckle in. Tuk's already there.

"Tell us about this storm, Tootega." I ask.

She appears in the dashboard lightscreen. "A category five cyclone, current coordinates indicate our location is directly in Uma's path."

"Help us out of here, Tootega!" I yell above the thundering rain.

There's a blinding flash of lightning and a deafening boom cracks the air, ringing in my ears. "Hello... hello... hello," I call out, unable to hear my voice as the instrument panel flickers. The ship rocks uncontrollably. We drop again and I scream.

Tuk squeezes my shoulder, "An extreme, rapid ascent is the only way to avoid Uma."

I nod quickly, my breath rapid and shallow.

"An extreme, rapid ascent to sixty thousand feet puts us above the cyclone," Tootega confirms, "but requires the pilot's assist on the control wheel."

I grab the wheel, my palms sweaty. Over the pounding in my ears, I shout, "Tell me when, Tootega!"

"Rapid ascent confirmed. Expect a force of five Gs for seven seconds."

The clouds go from gray to yellow to a sickening green, with rain and wind that pounds the ship so hard it roars, like a million booming drums. I can't even hear her when she says, "Now." But I watch her lips move and respond.

Pulling the control wheel toward me, fast and smooth, I slam back in the chair as we bolt through the storm like an emperor penguin rocketing out of the ocean. The world goes colorless as we level out at the edge of the stratosphere, where the atmosphere is smooth as glass, and the silence sacred. Uma spirals below like a furious, foaming galaxy.

I try to relax my grip, but my fingers are frozen. One by one, I peel them off the wheel, then shake the tension out.

"Well done, Luki!" Tuk beams and taps my shoulder. "I could not have performed that operation better myself."

I grin weakly. "How much time to get to Puerto Rico?"

"Assuming we travel at maximum speed, just under nine hours."

"Take over, would you? I'm going to lie down with Mig."

He smiles and his eyes crinkle. "I thought you would never ask!"

When I go to release Mig from his shelter under my bed, I smell poop; I'm glad he's shedding. His turds are easier to clean up when they're full of fur. I'll use Ssanibot to disinfect the cubby, later. I need to be horizontal. *Now.* I strip off my pants, pull off the foot, and crawl under the covers where I fall asleep, like dropping off a cliff...and dream.

I dream of an alabaster world where my parents are imprisoned behind bleached bars. In a brightly lit hall, a colossal, barefoot man brings them plates of food that he sets on the floor and slides under the bars with a fat toe. A thin, ugly man with long, white hair stands nearby in red pajamas holding a strange, scaly ball. Then the dream shifts.

I'm standing outside a house holding a gift. The door swings open and Korave pulls me inside, wraps his arms around me and bends to rub noses. His warm nose tickles. I feel myself slipping from the dream, but don't want to leave Korave. My nose tickles with something warm and wet. I crack my eyes. It's Mig, licking my nose and cheeks. I didn't feed him last night. He's hungry. I check my miniQ. It's five am.

Wiping my nose, I stretch. "Okay, boy. Let's get some food."

We keep voles and fish in the freezer for Mig, or endangereds my parents might rescue, and some caribou too. Digging three voles out, I drop them, clanking into his metal bowl under the galley table, and hear one of Nuwa's biggest hits float from the cockpit.

I lean in to discover Tuk lip syncing. But wait! He's not lip syncing. He's singing with her exact voice. "How do you do that?" I ask.

Tuk stops and whips around, "I contain all her songs, and her dance moves... and I concur with Frank and Virginia—Nuwa should sing one of your songs." He smiles. "It would naturally be a hit if she sang it and could change billions of minds. At least it might help slow the extinction."

"You're programmed with her dance moves? Show me!"

"In that case, I will need additional space... Tootega, assume control until my return." He unbuckles and I follow him into the galley.

"I shall sing, *'I Do Not Bow to You,'*." He starts and Nuwa's voice floats out of his mouth. "*I bow to truth, I bow to wisdom, but I do not bow to you...*"

This is Aana's absolute favorite song. He sings it perfectly, shaking his finger, swaying his hips, tilting his head... *just like her!* So weird! Like she's inside him and taken over his body. Like Tuk is a Nuwa zombie!

"*I do not bow to you, I do not bow to you, no never will I dooooooo... You left my heart in pieces, pieces. You left my heart in pieces!*"

He's got all her moves, and in her shrill soprano mimes tearing his heart out and ripping it up. Flawlessly!

I can't help but laugh. "She always sounds like a baby mammal crying... or dying... she's got to be a gynoid!"

For Nuwa to sing one of my songs... a song to save endangereds... a song to save thousands or millions... a song blasting around the world to help end the Sixth Extinction... it's irresistible. It wouldn't matter that I can't stand her.

Tuk ends with a bow.

"Bravo!" I clap. "I'd give you a standing ovation, but I'm standing already."

"I appreciate your enthusiasm, but I am engineered for mimicry. Not as remarkable as your mindsight and ability to perceive spiritcords."

Turning my head, a spiritcord flashes in my mindsight. "How soon before we're there?"

"Less than an hour."

I need to look at the island. "Tootega, activate the galley lightscreen with a map of Puerto Rico."

The spiritcord pulses, gleaming in my mindsight as the lightscreen in the wall above the 3-D printer flashes an island shaped like a rectangle.

"We should land here," I point to the southwest shore, "exactly where the spiritcord leads. Zoom in on my finger, Tootega."

The map reads, "Guanica State Forest."

"Of course, the Guanica Dry Forest," Tuk says. "Pablo decimated the island a year ago."

"Pablo?" I shrug. "Who's Pablo?"

"A category five hurricane. Thousands perished. The island never recovered. Landing will be a challenge."

"Start the descent and call me when we're at five thousand feet. Your Nuwa impression inspired me."

10
Antoadia and the Earwig

Tuk and I gaze out the galley window. We've landed on a tumble of limestone near the ruins of a lighthouse, the sapphire sea just beyond. The air sparkles, the sky crystal clear, but thanks to Pablo, it's like a bomb site. Mammoth cactus and uprooted trees are piled up like a heap of bones in a game of Inukat. Trails are impassable in the shredded forest.

"Unlock and open the galley exit, Tootega," I ask, suddenly dying to breathe fresh air.

"The proximity of vegetation causes an obstruction, which renders egress impassable. My sensors indicate... a massive cluster of Melocactus intortus." Tootega says.

Tuk adds, "Melocactus intortus from the flowering plant family Caryophyllales. It is a plump cactus ribbed with two-inch spikes with a thorny, red protuberance at its pinnacle, like a hat."

"Hardly mellow with those wicked thorns!" I snicker.

"And there, the amphibian hops!" Tuk exclaims. "Its olive green and gold skin camouflages it well among the organic debris."

"Do I need binocs?"

"Unnecessary." He points. "Straight ahead, twelve o'clock, the amphibian approximately six feet away..."

I hold my breath and focus on the rocks and chaos out there. Nothing.

Tuk's laser-like eyes never blink. "Preyed upon by mongoose and feral cats, many more toads died in the hurricane. The few that endured are extraordinary survivors, critically endangered."

Exhaling, I relax and scan. Finally, I catch a glimpse of something. "I think that's her."

"Without examination, how do you know the sex?" Tuk asks.

"I'm sensing feminine energy... Tootega, activate arm one." Pulling open the galley drawer, I shove my hand inside the glove.

Leaning across the table, my arm out-stretched, I extend the mechanical arm as far as it will go.

"Almost there." Tuk says.

"I can't get any closer," I say.

"Not close enough." He shakes his head.

Turning my palm, I spread the electronic fingers, resting the remote hand palm-up in the shade.

"There's nothing to fear," I whisper, my mind-message clear. "Jump," I say, transmitting an image of her sitting in the palm of the hand.

She jumps—away from the hand! Again, I move it towards her, but still not close enough.

"Come on." I sigh, frustrated.

She moves with an awkward walk-hop to the left, further away, and my arm starts to cramp.

Concentrating, I send the mind-message again, "Jump in the hand... there's nothing to fear... please."

A bug scuttles up from a rock and crawls between the fingers into the palm.

"The amphibian stalks prey!" Tuk declares, jolting my focus.

"What is that, anyway?"

He stares at the bug. "An earwig, order dermaptera, known for their characteristic forceps-like pincers protruding from the abdomen. Nocturnal insects, unusual to see one during the day."

The bug sits there. "Earwig? What a weird name! Maybe it adapted, like Mig?"

The bug rests motionless, except for its antenna swinging back and forth.

Tuk doesn't move a muscle, his eyes glued to it, "The name comes from a wives' tale that the insects crawled into people's ears, and burrowed into their brains to lay eggs..."

"Ew!"

"... and so widespread, they exist on every continent, except Antarctica..."

"I never saw one in Alaska....I never even knew they existed!"

The bug still isn't moving, and Tuk-who-knows-it-all goes on, like I *need* to know everything about the bug. "Most notable, females may care for their eggs, even after they hatch as nymphs. Female earwigs watch over their offspring until their second molt."

If he were human, I wouldn't believe him. "Motherly bugs? Seriously? *Very* weird!"

"Observe, Luki, the amphibian stalks the earwig."

The toad turns and walk-hops toward the hand. She takes two steps and stops. Then another, and another, straddling the fingers... and freezes. One more step. The bug's antennae stop moving. The toad lunges. In one lightning move, the earwig disappears, except for the tips of the butt pincers sticking out of the toad's mouth. She's in the middle of the palm now!

The toad stuffs the pincers in her mouth and as I pull the arm into the hatch, my mindsight receives a picture.

"I do not fear." She sends an image of her staring down a mongoose.

Twisting my arm around, I release the mechanical hand and drop her gently into the sink. She stares with round, yellow, unblinking eyes as I lift the mechanical hand dripping with her urine.

"Telling you true, I cannot help it." With a guttural croak, her voice pulses in my mind's ear like rhythmic waves. "Peeing happens during stressful situations," she sends a picture—of a cat lurking above the limestone crevice where she's hiding, in a teensy puddle of pee.

"Skillful job, Luki, though apparently her autonomic nervous system caused her to urinate."

"She said she was stressed." I reply and remove the glove.

"During hyperarousal, a fundamental reaction among vertebrates causes urination." Tuk pauses and stares at the ceiling. "No doubt she perceived the electronic arm as a threat, which activated her fight, flight or freeze response."

I sigh, "You need to analyze everything, don't you, Professor Omniscient?" I roll my eyes.

He looks surprised. "My system processes based on the six steps of Bloom's taxonomy, and the nature of learning and critical thinking." He numbers with his fingers. "First there is knowledge, second there is comprehension, third is application, followed by fourth, analysis, fifth, synthesis and sixth, evaluation."

I don't care how we learn or anybody's taxonomy. "Thanks for the lesson, Professor. Now do the toad a favor, grab some earth and a piece of bark, something for her to hide under...here." I toss the glove. "I'll get a larger vivarium from storage. Let's put Antoadia near the Slimendiggers so she has something to watch."

"Aye-aye, Captain. A clever name, Antoadia, like Professor Omniscient. Quite appropriate." He grins. "This reminds me of a crucial XH7 feature, of which you are likely aware."

"What?" I snap.

"I am programmed never to compromise." He smiles.

We're in the cockpit, buckled in, almost at cruising altitude. I'm setting approximate destination coordinates when Tuk turns to me.

"I considered and thoroughly processed a concept which involves landing in Romania, on the way to the Caucasus."

"Romania? What for?"

"A pig."

"What are you talking about?" My voice rises. "A pig was not part of the plan! Red Dragons want the critically endangered and the functionally extinct and pigs are neither!" I reply, glancing at the altimeter. We're at 63,000 feet.

Tuk clears his throat and shifts toward me. "The Mangalitsa pig was almost extinct once, although not endangered, many consider their flesh a delicacy. With human populations plummeting due to chemicals in the environment for over seventy years..."

He's really getting on my nerves. "Why does that matter, and how does that relate to the pig?"

"... through compounds from plastics, drugs and pesticides that affect humans and animals," he continues. "The Mangalitsa, like hundreds of amphibian species and like people around the world, has difficulty reproducing. Red Dragons are not such discriminating traffickers that White Wolf won't jump at the opportunity."

I focus on the dashboard and the compass. We're crossing the Atlantic, heading northeast toward Europe. "You think White Wolf is going to want a pig that's *not* endangered?"

"It took four point eight seconds for my system to process the six cognitive steps of Bloom's Taxonomy. I am confident we should proceed with this relatively minor detour."

It took him seconds to make this decision? I've agreed with everything, but a pig? Why did I ever go along with him to begin with?

"If we've got the endangereds he wants, I don't understand why we need a pig! And what about its food?" I whine.

"White Wolf will prize our exotic porcine breed. Presenting the Mangalitsa will enhance our legitimacy. With my agricultural skills, I shall grow its feed."

This entire operation is *his* idea! I agreed in the beginning, but do I even have a choice now? I must go along... he meant it when he said he never compromises, which means I *have* to!

"If you're so confident, and if it's that rare...." I sigh, giving in.

"And let us not forget," he raises a finger, "that meat eating humans love the taste of pork."

"I wouldn't know... I eat insects, mostly." I reply.

"Perhaps your outlook will improve if you were to locate a Mangalitsa that *required* rescue?"

I can't listen anymore and unbuckle. "You pilot. I'll learn about the breed, what it looks like and try to find one that needs saving."

"The Prof. is happy to pilot while you study the pig-sheep."

"Pig-sheep?!"

11
A Blonde Boar and Bison

The face of a fat pig with curly blonde fur stares at me from the lightscreen on the wall of my cabin. I'm lying on my bed so tired I can hardly keep my eyes open. I close them for a nano and a thick, spiritcord glows in my mindsight.

"Tootega, how much space does a full-grown pig need?" I ask, one eye cracked.

The pig's face dissolves and Tootega's appears. "Swine over 250 pounds require a minimum of ten square feet."

With a spiritcord so radiant and plump, it must weigh at least that much.

"Pull up a map of Eastern Europe. Zoom in and tell me this location." I ask, getting off the bed to stick my finger in the lightscreen where the spiritcord leads. "Keep zooming until I tell you to stop..."

She zooms in.

".... okay stop! Where is this?"

"Romania."

"Zoom an extra nano... okay, stop! Here," I say, pointing, the spiritcord beams in my mindsight.

"The village of Runcu in the Southern Carpathian Mountains, known as the Transylvanian Alps."

I shudder...I always thought Transylvania was pure fiction. I never knew the place actually existed! Does that mean vampires and werewolves are real too? I'm no superhero, but there's no turning back now. "Set destination coordinates for Runcu and prepare fauna room one with the most absorbent material in the system."

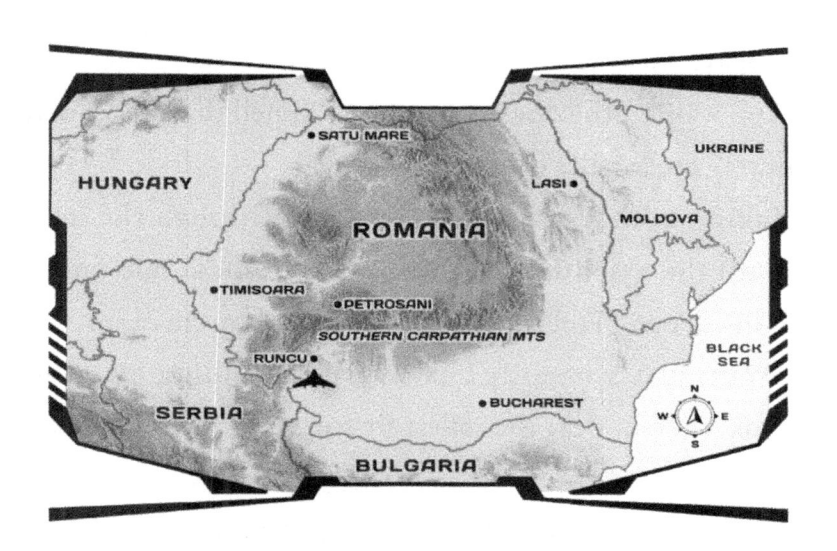

We touch down in a valley meadow, once farmland, now abandoned. Thick forests stud mountains on both sides of the valley. I'm still buckled, but as soon as the cargo door opens and the fresh air whooshes in, I want out. So does Mig—I feel it. Tuk waits while I go to release Mig.

Peering through the caged door in the cubby under my bed, I tell him, "Don't go far. Understand?" Before unlatching the cubby door, I send a picture of him at my side.

"Hungry!" He sends a picture of a fat vole as I release him.

"Come when I call you," I tell him.

"Okay!" he says as he bolts.

Tuk waits at the open cargo door. "Smell the old growth forest?" He inhales deeply.

Taking a whiff, I watch Mig zigzag through the field toward the woods. "It's crisp, smells fresh. Come on," I tug his sleeve. "Follow me," and head down the ramp.

"Wait, just a nano!" Tuk whispers, pulling my arm. "Look, there....near the tallest fir tree. Fifty-three yards at two o'clock."

My eyes dart to the edge of the meadow. Grazing under an enormous tree is a huge, blonde boar.

Mig gives the boar a wide berth and barks, "Stinks!" in my mind's ear, then trots into the woods beyond.

Tuk and I stop within ten feet of the boar. He lifts his head and snorts loudly. He's monstrous—big enough to ride, but who would dare? He's not cute, cuddly or clean, like the pictures and holograms. His coat is full of twigs and leaves, brambles, nuts and seeds. Shriveled berries, dirt and burrs cake his legs, and his belly is plastered with dried mud, like a layer of bark. Drooling, with twisted tusks and blonde, wavy ears that hang low over his eyes, he gives one deep grunt proclaiming, "I am found!" His voice slurps and sucks in my mind's ear, like pulling boots from the mud.

"I was the last one off," he grunts with a rush of pictures—of pigs crammed in the back of a truck, suffocating in a cloud of exhaust and ammonia fumes. Pigs, lined up in a row, prodded down a ramp into a labyrinth. Death by stun gun. Men in colorless coats slit pig throats. Blood flows in crimson channels. Headless pig bodies hang from overhead hooks.

Overcome, I shake the horrible images from my mindsight.

"I jumped into a bed of straw and ran. Ran for my life into the forest." He snorts.

I lean in to Tuk, "Stay here, I'll use my mindsight and get him to follow me." Approaching casually, I stoop to pick a red mushroom with white spots.

I send the pig a picture—of him walking behind me up the ramp, "Come, Hogman," I say and wave the mushroom under his nose. Frightened, he bolts but stops close to the ship to root on the ground.

I head back to Tuk.

"We must be patient," he whispers. "The porcine species does not respond well to being rushed. It is his nature. Not to mention that he is a herd animal, likely stressed from his time alone."

Curious, but reluctant to walk the ramp even after I spread acorns up into the hall, the boar continues to root in the grass.

"Isn't there something we can do?" I ask, feeling impatient.

"I shall activate the ramp lights. Brightly lit areas attract pigs," Tuk declares.

He disappears into the ship and a moment later the ramp glows. Tuk waits inside, holding the fauna door wide.

Finally interested, the boar plods lazily up the ramp, his ears flopping with every step, and heads into fauna room one. Inside the barred room, he farts and flops down. Tuk closes the door. The upper half of the door and wall to the hall has bars. Like vivariums, the bottom half of the door is electrochromic.

"Please bring a bowl of water," Tuk calls out. In the room, giant absorbent pellets, like super-sized macaroni cover the floor, ankle-deep.

I nod. "Meantime, give him this," and pass the mushroom through the bars. When I bring him a metal bowl filled with water, Tuk sets it in the far corner and eases out the door. We watch through the bars as the boar shuffles over and slurps, sloshing water everywhere. Instantly the absorbent pellets puff up to ten times their size.

"He's huge, Tuk!"

"A prize specimen!"

There's not enough food in the freezer or greenwall for the boar. "We don't have enough to feed him. Any brilliant ideas now?"

Like a magician, Tuk reaches into his pockets and pulls out his fists, displaying their contents. Two small nuts in one palm, two larger, nearly black nuts in the other. "Acorns and black walnuts," he declares triumphantly.

"You've got to be kidding. That's not even a snack for a piglet!"

"Ah sweet Luki, do not take these literally. I require merely a single cell from these kernels to produce an endless supply, as much as our boar demands."

"That's what you meant by agricultural skills? I wouldn't call lab food 'agriculture.'" I reply with air quotes. "He'll need soy and corn too, and I'll share berries and lettuce from the greenwall, but that'll never be enough."

"Do not worry. The seed vault contains whatever the boar requires."

The seed vault... Dad bought it when he installed the far moire... *at home.*

"The seed vault isn't here, it's at home, in Wales." A sad, sinking feeling washes over me. Mom... Dad... Home.

"My mindfile indicates your father divided the seeds, and placed a bucket in storage aboard the ship..."

"Really?" I step into the storage room, across the hall from Hogman.

"It shall produce plenty for the porker."

Tuk isn't like a magician, he *is* a magician. Occasionally, a super annoying one!

"There." He points to a sealed bucket on the floor in the corner, under the shelf of drones. "I shall begin lab food production while you retrieve your fox."

"Do you think Hogman should be cleaned?"

Tuk nods. "That name suits him well. And you are correct. Our samples must look presentable when we display them to White Wolf. The organic detritus should be removed. Perhaps you will have time to wash him when you return?" His eyes brighten.

The thought of scrubbing the filthy beast annoys me. The pig was his idea — he should clean it. "The cinereous vulture is next, right?"

"Correct. The Caucasus a mere two hours and fourteen minutes from here."

"I've got to learn about the vulture for my mindsight to detect the spiritcord. I'm heading to my cabin. The porker is yours to clean. After all, he was *your* idea."

"Very well. We shall clean the Mangalitsa after the cinereous vulture!"

That's what he thinks.

With Mig's and my favorite treat in my pocket— super nutty protein peanut butter cricket bars—I go down the ramp and wade through the high grass.

"Mig! Treat! Come Mig! Treat! Treat!" I shout into the stillness. The ancient trees tower overhead. Their thick, mossy roots look like gnarled fingers that reach out to hold hands with gnarly roots nearby. The forest floor is carpeted with dead leaves. Along the banks of a rushing stream, ferns unfurl like green feathers. I stop to sit on a mossy root and soak up the wisdom of these beautiful, sacred woods.

"Mig! Mig! Come on boy!" I shout again. I flash on Korave and check my miniQ. It's three thirty, which means it's.... tomorrow morning in Russia?

Questioning my wrist, I ask, "What time is it in Provideniya?"

"In Provideniya, center of the Providensky District of Shukotka Autonomous Okrug, Russia, it is one thirty-five am."

My mindsight flashes on Korave in bed, asleep, and I send him a picture—of me here on the moss, waving to him. "I miss you." I close my eyes and wait.

Seconds later Korave whispers in my mind's ear, "Luki—you are doing it!"

"I'm just going along with Tuk. I don't know what I'm doing," I shrug.

"You are one sharp doughnut." Sitting up in bed he taps his temple.

I sigh. "I wish you were here."

"Me, too. Mama knows you possess much *udachi* and wants to meet you. She says you must not fear." He fades from my mindsight.

"Don't go; please don't go."

There's a rumble, a low grunting deep in the woods. Ignoring it, my mind drifts back to Korave. I start to daydream about meeting his parents.

He's in a doorway and pulls me inside. "Meet Mama."

She squeezes my hand, pumping it up and down, smiling hard as strings of beads shimmy down her face from an intricate headdress. Faded tattood lines trails down her nose and chin. She points to a table set with forks, plates, teacups and in the middle, a layered cake. Droid legs, arms, hands and feet are scattered across the floor.

"Meet Papa," Korave says.

Like a grizzly bear, his swarthy father bends to kiss me on each cheek. A legless droid rolls by on a wheeled platform bearing a tray with a bottle and tiny glasses.

"Even with no legs, Lyosha is excellent help," Korave declares proudly while the droid pours, and gives the first glass to Papa.

Papa shouts, "Bóodeem zdaróvye,"[1] revealing the same gap-toothed smile Korave has, and chugs his drink in one gulp.

Lyosha hands me a glass.

Korave grins, nudging me. "Polite to drink when meeting."

---

1. Russian drinking toast, "To our health!"

I smile and chug like his father. The liquid burns as it slides down my throat. Korave takes my hand and leads me outside the back door. The night is frosty, the snow looks indigo in the moonlight. We wade through his caribou herd. The glowing aurora wavers across the sky. We're heading to his yaranga, the tent he's told me about, glowing orange like a lantern in the distance.

Korave holds the flap open for me. Caribou fur covers the walls and ground. A fire burns in a central pit. Korave throws sticks on the embers, and we huddle close for warmth. My head drops to his shoulder. The flames dance higher warming my hands and face. This den, his shelter, is pure bliss.

There's another grunt that rips me from my daydream. It's louder than Hogman's. *Much* louder. It reverberates like an alarm, and my heart skips a beat. I scan the woods. An immense furry head with small horns emerges from behind shrubs. Bison?! It grunts again and another appears even closer. *Bison!!*

"MIG!!!" I scream.

There's a flash of fluffy tail and a yelp. Mig emerges running, his snout bristling with quills.

Squatting as he nears, I offer a piece of cricket bar, but he's in too much pain. I try yanking a quill out but can't get a solid grip. My fingers keep slipping. The bison keeps grunting.

Are there more than two? Bulls defending territory or their harems?

Mindful of the quills, I gently lift Mig into my arms. The grunts get louder and closer. "Come on boy. We've got to get out of here. *Fast!* These woods belong to them." I break into a run.

"Good boy... what a good boy," I repeat, holding Mig's collar and stroking his back as he sits trembling on the galley table.

Tuk removes the quills with precision. His index finger and thumb wrap around each shaft and with a quick, firm yank, he extracts them one by one. In less than a minute he removes all eighteen.

"Your fingers are like pliers! Mine could never grip like that." I dab at Mig's snout with BLT—benzocaine, lidocaine, tetracaine—the triple anesthetic from the galley's first aid drawer. My parents use BLT on wounded endangereds all the time.

"How about a cricket bar now?" He eats it in two bites, jumps off the table, and scampers down the hall.

"XH7's contain setae on their palms and fingers, an advanced feature for the digits on my hands and feet." He holds out his hands. "They cover my palms and fingers, the soles of my feet and bottom of my toes."

"Setae?" I ask, pulling his wrist closer, staring without knowing what I'm looking for.

"Miniscule hair-like structures with thousands of much tinier spatulate formations covering them. My hands and feet contain millions, like geckos and worms."

I grin. "You can climb walls?!" I rub my fingers over his palm that feels a bit rough and sticky.

He nods, almost bashful. "Although the opportunity has never arisen."

"I'd love to watch you try!"

"Perhaps the occasion will occur during our mission?"

We'll be in serious trouble if he's got to climb walls. "I sure hope not." And head into the hall.

"Shall I pilot to the Caucasus then?"

"Yeah," I nod before heading to my cabin. "I'll tell Tootega to set destination coordinates once I've got the vultures' spiritcord in my mindsight."

12
Vomit Shots for the Vulture

"Known as the black vulture, monk vulture, or Eurasian black vulture, the cinereous vulture is one of the two largest Old-World vultures, growing to a maximum of thirty pounds, standing almost four feet tall, with a wingspan over ten feet." Tootega states.

Images of an immense bird appear on the lightscreen. Out of nowhere, my stomach hurts, like I've eaten something bad, and a dull spiritcord appears in my mindsight.

Clutching my belly, I roll off the bed. "Tootega, show me where we are on a map."

The spiritcord dims. Feel like I need to throw up, but I only ate a cricket bar. Must be feeling sympathetic pain for the vulture. Wherever she is, she's incredibly sick.

The vulture dissolves on the lightscreen and a map appears. "Where is this?" I stick my finger in the lightscreen where the spiritcord leads.

"Chugush, highest mountain in the Adygea, in the Western Caucasus."

"Set destination coordinates here," I whisper, and crawl back to bed, doubled over with pain.

Sunlight streams through my porthole as we glide from the troposphere into the stratosphere above Turkey and the inky waters of the Black Sea. The vulture's spiritcord fades from my mindsight and the pain disappears as I doze off wondering if we're too late.

A wall of nimbostratus clouds hides the sun when we touch down in the late afternoon and Tuk announces on the intercom, "At an elevation of 10,980 feet, we have landed above the tree line in the Nature Biosphere Reserve with a clear view of Chugush."

Mig jumps off the bed as I roll over and swing my legs over the side. I feel weak. I'm not ready. At this altitude I'm dizzy and nauseous with an instant headache. But the vulture is sick and can't wait. We've got to go *now*.

"Get the first aid kit. I'll get WEFT out of storage." I shout down the hall, heading toward the Wearable Emergency Faunal Transport. "Meet me at the ramp."

With a whoosh of hydraulics, *Anniqsuqti's* cargo ramp descends, making a high-pitched buzz that hurts my ears. With the scent of fresh pine and rotting fruit, the frigid air outside rushes into the stale air inside.

Mig trails me down the stairs to storage. I grab the WEFT from the shelf and my jacket from a hook. Tuk waits at the edge of the cargo ramp in his t-shirt with the first aid kit belted at his waist. Immediately I think he should wear a jacket.... but...he's a droid. They like it frosty.

In the sunset's peachy glow, Mig holds his head high, drinking in the air, his snout twitching. My breath forms a vapor cloud as a dull pain swirls in my belly. I don't know which is worse—altitude sickness or the vulture's poisoning? Closing my eyes, I inhale the icy air, but can't seem to catch my breath.

"OOHU, OOHU, OOHU." An owl calls through the trees below.

My eyes flash wide and a knife-like pain stabs me. "We've got to get going. She's still alive. Come on!" Mig sticks to me like a burr as we make our way over steep, snowy rocks before reaching the tree line and entering woods.

Inside the forest, Tuk stops to gaze up at the outline of an enormous owl, the biggest owl *ever*, watching us with orange eyes that seem to glow.

"What owl species is it?" I whisper over Tuk's shoulder.

"Bubo bubo." He whispers.

The silliest Latin name *ever*!

Tuk adds, "Eurasian eagle owl."

The owl rotates her head. She's tracking Mig, who's up ahead sniffing the ground. I sense she's hunting and whisper, "Tell me what they eat."

Like reading a grocery list, Tuk whispers, "Voles, rats, rabbits, woodpeckers, herons, amphibians, reptiles, fish, insects and sometimes," he pauses, "foxes."

I gasp softly. Mig's only seven pounds!

Mig sends a picture of the owl strapped to my back in the WEFT. He thinks we've come to rescue *this* bird.

I shake my head, "No," and send a picture of a cinereous vulture.

The owl drops from the tree all at once, in a smooth, high-speed swoop. Her wings span is at least six feet across and her feathered claws swell, spreading wide like grappling hooks aimed at Mig! Terrified, he leaps toward me. With a rush of adrenaline, I jump up, swinging my arms to fend off the huge raptor as Tuk collapses into a squat, shielding his head with his arms.

"No!" I shout as a wingtip brushes my face with the crisp scent of pine. Tail feathers swipe the top of my head, spin across my nose and whip past my eyes. I swing at it again and send the raptor into a somersault. Regaining her balance, she flies off weaving between the trees and disappears down the mountainside.

The encounter leaves me breathless. I squat to hug Mig, cowering at my feet. "That was close!"

Tuk stands. "Did you observe the avian dodge the trees as it flew off? Such an expert flier!"

"Did you observe she was about to kill Mig?" Hugging him tight, we're both panting. "And those massive claws!"

He nods wide-eyed. "I witnessed your deft handiwork when you swatted the tail feathers, which caused the massive bird an aerial wobble, from which it effortlessly recovered. Remarkable! Do you realize the entire encounter took less than three seconds?"

"Is that all? It felt like three minutes!" My body goes limp with relief.

"Time expanded for you during an extraordinary, human-animal encounter."

"An encounter I never want in Mig's life again!"

Fat, fluffy flakes starts to fall and stick to the ground.

"Come on." The vulture's spiritcord pulses weakly into the forest below. "Let's keep going."

After a ten minute descent through thick trees and dead branches, we come upon the snowy outline of a black form slumped on the ground against a tree trunk. Standing almost four-feet tall, her neck feathers stick out like a collar. Fuzzy down covers the top of her head and the back of drooping neck.

"Behold the aegypius monachus, family Accipitridae, order, falconiformes, class, aves, largest bird of prey on earth. She does not look at all well." Tuk says.

"She's been poisoned."

"We must make her purge."

We approach, crouching. She smells terrible—worse than Aanas' muktuk.

Falling faster, the snow, like cotton balls starts to coat everything. Tuk kneels and unzips the first aid pouch.

"Vomit shots are inside the second or third fold," I say, without taking my eyes off the raptor.

"Do you refer to the emetic syringes filled with ipecac?" he asks, unfolding the kit.

I nod. "Hurry!"

Endangereds almost always need what I call vomit shots to make them puke whatever they've ingested—poison or plastic.

He pulls out a syringe and uncaps it. "You will need to grasp her neck."

With both hands, I clasp her limp neck gently, but firmly.

Syringe in one hand, Tuk pries open her massive, hooked beak and, squirts the shot down her throat. She has no strength to resist. Is it enough? Dad used one syringe on gyrfalcons and eagles half her size.

With my hands still around her neck, my stomach cramps. "She might need another."

Tuk takes out a fresh syringe, cracks her beak again, and squirts. Snow collects on her shoulders and back.

Tuk pulls the stethoscope out, plugging the tips into his ears. As I brush the snow from her shoulders, he nestles the diaphragm through her breast feathers.

"Anything?" I ask.

He moves the diaphragm up, then down, burrows it closer to her skin, staring up at me, but not really seeing me.

"Anything?" I ask again.

"I'm getting a faint, irregular heartbeat. She may be in the throes of death."

"She should puke any second now." I am not giving up on this bird.

"If she fails to vomit, we must find another live specimen *somewhere*." Tuk rolls up the stethoscope and stows it in the kit.

"Let's leave her alone."

We go to wait under a nearby fir tree. It's almost dark. The woods are nearly soundless, except for the falling snow. Kneeling between Mig and Tuk, I watch for any sign of life. The ipecac should work by now.

"OOHU, OOHU, OOHU." My head whips around to the eagle owl's call, and just then, the vulture heaves a foul mass, as the ship's automatic headlights flash on beaming through the trees.

She's alive!

Like icy crystals, the vulture's thought-pictures sting my face. *"Wolf carcass taste nothing like rotting flesh I adore. Once we were safe... but... humans poison foxes...wolves...my mate, my nest, my egg...gone, gone, gone."* She slumps forward, opens her beak and.... *b*urps?!

"Let's be quick and spread the WEFT out over there." Nudging Tuk, I point to a spot between the trees.

It's snowing harder as we lay the smart fabric on the ground and prepare the system of flaps.

"I shall position her in the WEFT but require your assistance to wrap her."

"Of course!" I reply.

"I am thrilled to wear a cinereous vulture on my back!" Tuk compresses the wings against her body, lifting her into the middle of the WEFT.

Crouching, I pull the right flap over her body, attach the Velcro strip on the left, and repeat doing the opposite with the left flap. It's a good, snug fit.

"Like putting on a sleeveless coat."

"I enjoy fresh experiences." He grins.

"We've got to stand up now."

Inches apart, we face each other.

"Okay, turn around, and bend over at a ninety-degree angle, keep your hands on your knees and your back totally flat."

Tuk follows my instructions. "Perfect. Don't move. I'll put her on your back."

My hands crawl in the snow under the WEFT until I reach her body, hold firmly and lift. She's heavier than I expected, but motionless while I position her in the middle of Tuk's back with the WEFT hanging down his sides. Once his arms are through the holes and he knots the fabric against his chest, he can straighten.

"Okay, you can stand up now."

Tuk pulls the fabric taut across his shoulders. "Excellent instructions, Luki. The raptor is quite secure. I feel like an Eskimo mother with a baby in her papoose. Surely, I must look like one, do I not?" He smiles.

"Oh yeah! Exactly!" I burst out laughing. "...an Eskimo mother... with her beautiful baby vulture!"

"I detect your sarcasm, which I will ignore because I am enjoying the sensation of a raptor swaddled on my back." He closes his eyes.

"Let's go," I tug his arm. "Lead the way."

Following him through the trees, I find a stick to use as a perch for the vulture who I'll name Buzzie. She goes in the room next to Hogman.

Back on the ship, after wedging the branch low to the ground in a corner, we open the WEFT. Tuk lifts, grasping her as I try to wrap her talons around the branch. She can't do it. The talons on her right can't grip firmly, and there's no strength in her left. Her head droops as Tuk props her against the wall. We leave her and observe from the hall.

"Let us hope the avian survives the night." Tuk comments.

"My stomach hasn't cramped since she threw up."

"A positive indication."

"I think she'll be okay, and maybe she'll be hungry in the morning. We still have plenty of voles we can microwave."

"Distant cousins to Mongolian marmots, which her diet would include. Voles are quite distant, but cousins nevertheless." He grins.

"It's all we've got." I shrug.

"On the bright side, they do not carry fleas with bubonic plague." He smiles.

"Ew!" I turn to climb the spiral stairs. "I'm going to feed Mig and catch a couple of crickets for Antoadia. Let's stay here for the night."

"You need to learn about the African wild dog, and while you sleep on top of the world, I shall work in the lab producing feed for the boar who still requires cleaning."

"That's a morning chore with Ssanibot, before takeoff."

"Another fresh experience." He smiles.

"For *you* and Hogman!"

The setting sun streaks across the sky, silhouetting Chugush outside the galley window. Mig's pushing his bowl across the floor licking every bit of fur and vole. Grabbing a couple of strawberries, I head to bed. As I pull my braid apart, a golden plume with tan stripes floats to the floor—the ultimate eagle owl souvenir.

13
Totipotent Cells and Ssanibot

I'm bringing Buzzie three voles thawed from the microwave when Tuk steps out of the lab.

"What a productive night!" He gushes. "Once I extracted the totipotent cells from the organic matter of the nuts, and adjusted the ratios of nitrogen, phosphorus, potassium, zinc, iron, manganese, copper, boron and micro-nutrients, I accelerated the growth process with the advance sequence booster and voila!" He lifts a metal bucket of mush.

"Sounds complicated." I reply with my eyebrows raised.

"It is really quite simple." He reaches for Hogman's door. "The appropriate mix of corn, soy and nuts."

"That looks like enough to keep Hogman happy...at least for breakfast," I say.

Snorting with excitement, Hogman buries his head in the slop before Tuk sets the bucket down.

"He loves it!" Tuk's teeth gleam in the bright light. His smile dims when Hogman farts. In seconds the stink drifts into the hall, where Tuk hurries to join me.

"The boar produces malodorous methane." He crinkles his nose.

"There's no escaping it," I reply, holding my nose. I enter Buzzie's room, hugging the bowl of voles to my chest.

She sends me a picture of flies swarming an emaciated carcass rotting in a field — a sure sign she's hungry!

"*Ah, the stink... of the not so freshly dead...*" Buzzie squawks. "*A beast putrefying for three days.... delectable!*"

Dipping her beak into the bowl, she devours the Mongolian marmots' distant cousins in seconds. Whole.

Holding the Ssanibot, I stand outside Hogman's room showing Tuk how to use it. "Put your hand around the back," I spread my fingers. "It forms to your hand when you squeeze. But like Mom always told me, don't squeeze too hard!"

"Might it explode?"

I nod with a grin. "Just like the giant African snail! And if you break it, *everything* on board this ship will need cleaning by hand. Including Hogman."

Turning Ssanibot on, I push the button for manual mode and pass it to Tuk. "It's all yours."

"Modeled after scotoplanes—commonly called the sea pig from the genus of deep-sea cucumbers, Ssanibot's large spongy body has a main cleaning orifice on its underside. In manual mode its antennas and legs do not activate as it has no need for propulsion. When I move Ssanibot over the filthy boar, hundreds of its super-absorbent micro tendrils will move in and out of the cleaning orifice."

"Yep."

"Ssanibot slurps, sucks, and sanitizes in less than half the time of ordinary cleaning bots," and adds, "the double S means it's super!" He says with a goofy grin mimicking the commercial.

"You've got it," I grin, patting him on the shoulder. "I'll focus my mindsight on the African wild dog's spiritcord, while you and Ssanibot enjoy a fun, fresh experience."

The boar is all but buried in the absorbent bedding pellets. Tuk enters, sweeping the bloated bits aside with his feet. He switches on the Ssanibot, places it on Hogman's belly and works the bot back and forth.

Hogman sends a picture of a mud puddle and snorts, *"Wallowing!"*

"Thanks, Tuk," I say with two thumbs up.

He looks about as happy as the pig, grinning and nodding. I'm just glad I'm not the one sucking the muck from Hogman's fuzzy gut.

14
Termites and the African Wild Dog

We're cruising silently at 500 feet during our descent into Tanzania and the Serengeti. Tuk pilots. I'm in the galley snacking and looking out the window at the grassy plain swarming with wildebeests, zebras, giraffe and gazelle. The painted dog's spiritcord stretches shimmering miles into the distance.

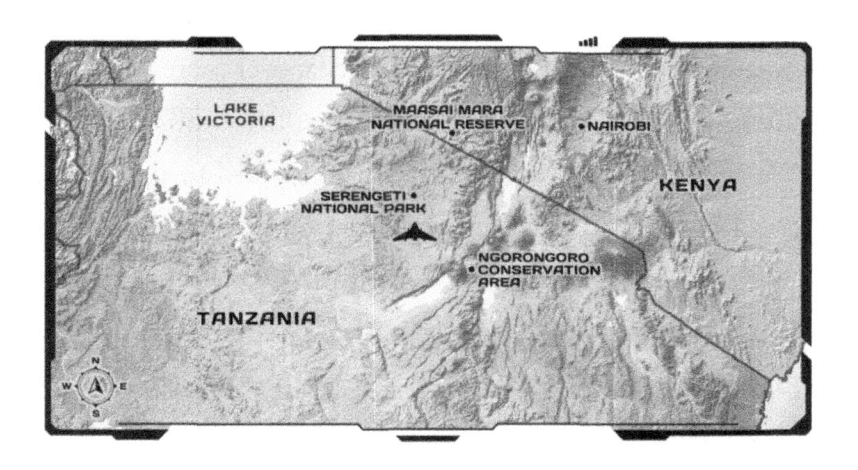

"Audio, Tootega—what are the brown circles in the earth below?"

"The northern Serengeti contains many termite mounds. Some reach seventeen feet," she states.

"Are termites edible?" I ask, biting into a drippingly ripe strawberry.

"Termites taste sweet, with a flavor like pineapple. Driver ants consume them."

I never tasted pineapple before. "Hmm, maybe I'll catch a couple."

"Use caution," she warns.

"I'm not afraid of termites."

"I refer to the ants."

"I'm not afraid of them either."

Heading to the cockpit, I buckle in for the landing. "Land us near the tree, the one like an umbrella, over there." I point.

"Adjacent to Acacia tortilis," Tuk says, "the umbrella tree."

We touch down. My shoulder burns. Hard to unbuckle. Can't move my upper arm without feeling a deep burning sensation.... it's the dog...it's *his* wound.

I release the harness, "I'm leaving Mig in his cubby."

"Excellent idea. We are vulnerable to one of Africa's apex land predators."

"Humans?"

He shakes his head. "Lions. We must not spend any more time here than absolutely necessary."

My stomach drops as I squeeze out between the seats. "Right." My mindsight's been so focused on the wounded wild dog, I never thought about getting attacked by *lions!*

"I'll bring the acoustigun, just in case." I unlock the drawer-safe, and stuff the two parts in my boots.

"Nevertheless, you are correct about humans," Tuk says. "You are apex predators, super-predators in fact, unique in your ability to influence ecosystems."

"Only in the worst possible way!"

He grabs the first aid kit from the drawer and belts it. "Your species is the entire reason for the sixth extinction."

"Don't you think I know that? Humans are so stupid!" My mouth droops, like Moms. "Tootega, audio—prepare room three with bedding for a dog; unlock and open the cargo door."

"Confirming canine bedding material and cargo egress."

"Let's go." Listening for the whoosh of the cargo door, I head to the aft stairs.

The cargo ramp kicks up a cloud of dust as it slides out. Scanning the primal grassland, I inhale the hot, feral air. The umbrella tree stands about a hundred yards ahead. There's nothing but grass for miles, shadowed by storm clouds in the distance. The dog's spiritcord runs in a straight line through the grass and around the tree.

"Where now?" Tuk asks, standing too close.

"His shoulder's hurt. He's up ahead near the tree."

Cautiously, I wade past termite mounds through grass growing to my knees. It's the rainy season here. Tuk spots him when we're thirty feet away.

"Eleven o'clock. In the shade, at the base of the trunk. He's licking his shoulder."

My eyes dart to the insects buzzing in the air. A mound of flies swarm across the wild dog's shoulder and a small cloud of flies buzzes above him. His ears are large and round, notched with scars. His eyes shine with intelligence. His bear-shaped head and cheeks are covered with light brown fur. A streak of black runs the length of his snout between his eyes, pointing to a bald muzzle. His mistrust engulfs me.

He stands on wobbling legs and sends me a blurred image... a man with a rifle. *"Back! Stay back!"* His voice thunders in my mind's ear, like hooves stampeding on dry, crusty earth.

My mind is clear and focused, my heart soft and open. I send him a picture—of him running free and happy with his pack. "We want to help you."

He sniffs the air, sending pictures that scatter in my mind-sight. *"Pack hunts. Running miles. Chasing wildebeest. Zebras panic. Antelope bolt. Blinding dust. Circle sick one. Hyenas close."* His nostrils flare, inhaling our scent.

His chest and belly swirl with black and brown fur that twirls down his spotted legs, like Aana's marble cake. He's beautiful.

"Bang! Bang, bang! Farmer. Poacher. Game hunter. Bloody pack. Running. Falling. In all directions." The violent images whirl like a dust storm through my mindsight.

He turns his head to the sky and howls. He waits, listening. He howls again and waits some more. And we wait, listening for an answer, from somewhere in this vast grassland, from out in his savanna. He waits for a howl from his pack to let him know they're alive still.

"Ooooooo…" comes a faint, birdlike reply, his ears turn, and he lies down again.

Closing my eyes, I send a picture—he's healed and strong, looking out across the plain.

His reply comes emphatically in sharp twitters. *"Humans over-breed. No room to hunt. Too hot to hunt. TOO HOT!"*

"We need to move in now," Tuk whispers. "He has lost a great deal of blood."

"He's less afraid." I nod.

Tuk says, "Weaker as well."

I sink softly to my knees. Kneeling on the dog's other side, Tuk opens the kit and removes a tube of numbing agent.

"Triple anesthetic BLT, a first aid essential." He whispers, unscrewing the cap, waving his hand over the flies to scatter them, if only for a moment.

Tuk squirts the BLT in and all around the wound. The blood seeps from the hole in the dog's shoulder but he doesn't move. Almost immediately my shoulder feels better. Tuk waits a minute, wipes the fur around the bullet hole with a sterile pad, and opens a pack of forceps. Staring at the bloody hole, he inserts the forceps straight in, with precision and extracts a bullet, straight out. Blood flows faster. Flies land on the blood trickling down the dog's shoulder. Placing the bloody forceps back in their pack, Tuk grabs a tube of Extra Cellular Matrix.

"Don't squeeze hard," I warn.

Squeezing half the tube, he squirts a huge blob in the bloody hole and, with his index and middle finger, spreads the goo around the wound. "His blood coagulates as ECM turns blue and hardens. The elasticity of the matrix keeps the wound closed and prevents infection." He wipes his fingers on a sterile pad and closes the kit.

Hooves stampede in my mind's ear abruptly, and an image of the dog staring down a warthog appears in my mindsight.

The dog opens his mouth showing fang-like teeth and makes a bird-like twittering sound.

"Is he telling you something meaningful?" Tuk asks.

"I don't know. He sent a picture of a warthog. I got the feeling he spied for his pack, that he's a sleuth. That's what we should call him—Sleuth! Let's give him space. I'll try to get him to follow me."

Tuk backs off. "Sleuth, the sly scout of his pack."

"Come," I say out loud, and send a picture—of him walking behind me in the grass.

He doesn't move, not a muscle, as the flies return, crawling up his leg and around the blue ECM. I send the identical picture again, and again, but he just lies there.

"He requires motivation of some kind," Tuk suggests.

My stomach growls. Of course, he's hungry! I send a picture of bloody meat in a bowl. He still doesn't move.

"I'll get caribou from the freezer." I turn, but don't see the ship anywhere! It's totally gone! "Where's the ship?!" I scan the grassland but all I see is grass, sky and termite mounds.

"*Anniqsuqti* is gone!" I gasp.

Calmly Tuk explains, "The angle of the sun's reflection on the quantum stealth cloak renders the ship entirely invisible. You must relax your eyes to identify its contours. You will see it clearly when you observe the grass and distinguish the unnatural lines of the vegetation created by the weight of the ship bearing down upon it.

Softening my focus, I scan the savanna for a shape that's grass but not grass... grass that's sharply angled... bent... unnatural grass.... and... there...I detect what must be the ship's wing—a stretch of grass bent at an odd angle. I take off and race up the ramp into the galley where I dig out several chunks of frozen caribou from the freezer and toss them in the microwave until the blood starts to seep. Running back with the bowl, I find Tuk guarding the dog.

Tuk says, "It may not be wildebeest, but its ungulate cousin is genetically close enough to satisfy his hunger. Feed him one chunk at a time. I shall follow behind as he moves."

Catching the scent of the meat, the dog sits up, his nose twitching. Creeping close, I throw a bloody chunk on the ground in front of him. Gone in one bite. Taking several steps back, I throw another chunk a little further away. He hops forward on three legs. This too is gone in a single bite. His mouth is enormous, his dagger-like teeth are made for ripping. The bowl is empty and we're only halfway to the ship. An earthen mound rises beside us with three globular stacks, at least twelve feet tall—a termite mound. Sleuth sits, waiting for another chunk of meat. Tuk stands six feet behind him.

I kneel for a closer look at the base of the mound.

"What are you doing?" Tuk asks.

"Looking for termites."

"Why?" he asks.

"To see what pineapple tastes like."

"Yes, but why now?" he wants to know.

"Because I've never tasted it before!"

He walks a wide circle around the dog and kneels beside me.

At the edge of the mound, a stream of brown ants race from a hole with termites on their heads.

I'm fascinated. "They're like thieves sprinting with stolen treasure!"

"Precisely!"

Dozens of ants rush out fast.

Tuk stares at the hole. "Any moment now, look for soldier termites with enormous heads, hooked jaws, and razor teeth. Watch for them to lunge and scissor their mandibles on the attack."

Ant heads fall, one by one, as the termites behead and dismember any ant in their way.

"Mandibles with the exactitude of miniscule guillotines!" Tuk declares.

"Ew… they're intense…. and ouch… ouch!" My ankle stings… and stings again… and again. A line of ants is crawling into my boot!? Swiping them away, I pull my boot off.

"I do not comprehend why they should have any interest in you," Tuk says.

Three ants dig their jaws into the skin above my ankle, biting hard. I whisper-yell, "I don't know either!" Pinching their abdomens, I pull, ripping them in half. Like tiny staples, their jaws embed in the stain that must have dribbled from the strawberries I ate. "I can't pull them out!"

Tuk leans in for a close look. "Their jaws will require extraction with tweezers. Tribal people use these ants to staple their wounds when injured. Quite remarkable."

Squinting in disbelief, I ask, "They *force* the ants to bite them?"

He nods knowingly. "Like ew, ouch and wow. Right?"

I nod, shaking my boot, check for ants inside, lean on Tuk's shoulder and pull it back on. "Let's get out of here before the *real* apex predators show up."

"Give me the bowl. I shall retrieve more." Tuk sprints through the grass, and returns with enough meat to coax Sleuth, hopping on three legs, up the ramp and onto the ship.

Mig barks from his cubby.

"Perhaps Mig feels threatened by the African wild dog," Tuk suggests as we watch Sleuth explore his room.

"Jealous is more like it," I reply.

15
A Dehydrated Tortoise

Mig gekkers a duet with Sleuth as soon as I release him. Gekkering is a combination of stuttering yelps, howls and rattles. Sleuth chirps back. Meanwhile, Tuk pries the ant jaws from my leg, and Mig ignores the pictures I blast to try and quiet him. Pictures of him on my lap, on my bed curled at my feet; me feeding him, playing with him, petting him, hugging him. Finally, I yell, "STOP!" Eventually he quits, but only after I'm in the cockpit and he curls on my lap, knowing that I'm still his.

We're on our descent toward the Mozambique Channel. It makes no sense, but this is where the spiritcord leads, the one that belongs to a radiated tortoise.

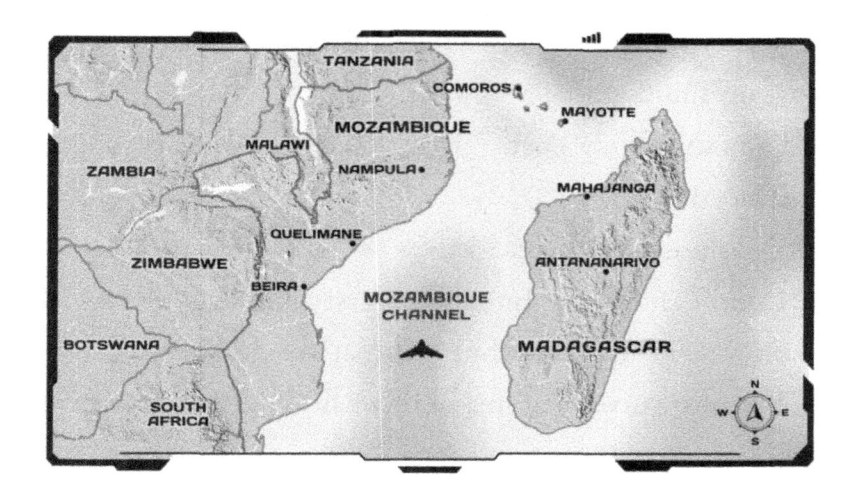

As we approach the azure waters, my mouth and throat get really dry. I start coughing and can't stop, coughing Mig off my lap. Tuk unbuckles and heads to the galley for water.

"Thanks," I whisper, sipping, but my throat still feels bone dry.

Tuk squints. "I find it most odd that your mindsight located a tortoise on this stretch of the Indian Ocean between Mozambique and southeast Africa."

"Spiritcords don't lie, and *this* is where it leads."

Like wind choked with sand, there's a hissing in my mind's ear. A voice that's low and sultry says, *"Humans took my freedom.... held me captive...hot and crowded in a pen...with dozens of my kind...I became a companion for those that live on the sea...what happened to the others I don't know...we are the most beautiful...*" The voice trails off as the spiritcord melts from my mindsight.

"She's somebody's pet..." I say, "on a boat... but her spiritcord faded."

"Did she expire?" Tuk asks.

"I don't think so... but she's thirsty and dehydrated." I swallow painfully. "It's why my throat's so dry!"

"We must survey the area until we find the coordinates of this boat."

"Definitely." But I worry we won't make it in time. Something is very wrong.

Cruising for hours, we scrutinize every square mile on an invisible grid.

Firelight fills the sky and turns the cockpit orange when the sun dips below the horizon. I blink, lifting the binoculars, my eyes almost as dry as my throat. "See that speck? It could be the boat...it could be her."

"Where?" Tuk asks, scanning the water.

"Between nine and ten o'clock. Tootega, reduce speed. I'll bring us down to twenty feet above the water for a closer look."

Tuk stares, squinting at the water. "That speck is a tangled mass of plastic netting. Like a magnet, it attracts more plastic.

Tentacles of the petrochemical plague foul every waterway. From micro particles in the atmosphere, to the deepest ocean trenches and the highest mountains, the plastic pandemic is omnipresent on earth."

"I could barf!"

"Truly?" Tuk's eyes widen.

Why would he doubt that? "Yes!"

"Interesting."

"What is so interesting about *that*?"

"That a mere fact could upset your digestive system and elicit vomitous."

I nod.

"In that case, the petro-chemical plague is likely *the* most nauseating aspect of the Anthropocene." He grins, then says. "Eyes on two o'clock. There appears to be a boat."

Lifting the binocs, I see it in the dusky light. "Yes!"

"It seems adrift," Tuk says as we draw closer.

Her spiritcord flickers in my mindsight as I scan the yacht. "She's on that yacht!" I lower the binocs. "But I don't see anyone on deck."

"Nor do I. Perhaps there has been an abduction?"

"Abduction?" I ask.

"Pirates find haven in this channel."

My heart flutters, and gasp. "Pirates?" Who knew pirates still existed?! "We're getting that tortoise and flying out of here. Fast!"

We cruise to the yacht, and hover above it. "Activate arm one, Tootega," I order.

"Arm one activated," she confirms.

"Maintain hover, Tuk. I'm going to retrieve her."

He cocks his neck at an odd angle as he studies the boat. "The tortoise sits on a pile of netting—in the aft."

"Take us to the aft, close enough for the arm to reach her."

Unbuckling, I lurch out of my seat and head to the galley, where I pull on the glove.

Maneuvering the mechanical arm down to her is easy enough, but the light is dim and each time I wrap the fingers around her shell, they catch on the netting.

"Do not grasp underneath to her scutes," Tuk shouts from the cockpit. "Grip only the dome of her carapace."

Eyes on the mechanical hand, I reach down and push the suction cup fingertips onto the top of her shell, I grip firmly and pull. Her head and legs droop lifelessly below the shell as I lift. But something's wrong. I can't raise her more than a couple inches.

"She's stuck!" I shout.

Suddenly beside me, Tuk says, "Try moving her back and forth to pry her foot loose."

Doing as he instructs; gradually I manage to free her. Slowly, I raise her into the hatch, where Tuk receives her on board.

"Dehydrated, indeed," he says and places her on the table. She's so weak, her legs sprawl. He opens the first aid drawer and starts rummaging.

"Is there a fetal Doppler?"

"Check the bottom drawer."

"Yes!" He holds it triumphantly. "The singular way to detect a heartbeat." He places the probe under the top of her shell, on the skin above her arm.

We wait for numbers to appear on the mini screen. After a minute, there's a single number—six.

"Six heartbeats in sixty seconds? That's *nothing!*"

"Her heartbeats should be closer to ten per minute," he says and pinches the skin on her legs. "She requires ultra-hydrating, transdermal patches."

I dig out a large adhesive patch from the drawer. "Mom and Dad used these to treat sick seals, polar bears or walrus."

"Too large." He scowls.

"I'll cut it." I grab the scissors and cut the patch in half. "She barely has any skin."

"We shall wrap her legs. Cut those in half again. You cover the front legs; I shall swaddle the back."

She looks like a mummy by the time we're finished. Absorption takes fifteen minutes. We wait and watch. Gradually, miraculously, she comes to life—one eye, then the other opens. She transmits pictures, crystal clear... with that sultry voice, like whirlwinds hissing across dunes in my mind's ear.

"Thank you for saving me from that hideous, stinking vessel. I was doomed by asphyxiation, and the stench of rotting fish. I got caught. Couldn't move. Not that I didn't try... desperately I wanted to crawl into a corner, out of the sun. But impossible. My legs...like stone....and my nails..." she lifts her front leg, *"got stuck..."*

Pointy claws curve from her foot.

"I had no strength to pry them loose from that horrid tangle, the sun cooking me in that hole, hot as Hades." She closes her eyes and pumps her legs.

"I'm in a puddle... after the monsoon..." she swoons.

"She is extraordinarily beautiful with a carapace so highly domed she is nearly round." Tuk runs his finger across her back. "And her nuchal scute, above her head, has an unusual flare."

"She's a gem! Her yellow starbursts are like golden snowflakes swirling on a winter night! We should name her Allia."

"A perfect Inupiaq name," Tuk says. "Did you notice the stunning starburst design on her carapace radiates below her scutes?"

Nodding, I tear a few lettuce leaves and pick a ripe strawberry.

"The berry's vitamin C is precisely what the reptile needs. I shall take her to faunal room four." Tuk lifts the top of her dome with his sticky fingertips, her wrapped legs dangling.

I've never experienced an actual reptile before and want to stay with her. "How about you look at a map and find a quiet cove to anchor for the night while I take her down?"

"I know where we should stay," he says, passing her to me.

Cradling her against my belly, she bites at the strawberry ravenously. "Show me, Tuk. Tootega, pull up a map of the Mozambique Channel."

A map appears in the small galley lightscreen above the 3-D printer.

"Mayotte, oldest of the Comoros archipelago," he points to a speck in the water. "Zoom in, Tootega. We are safest close to the volcanic island in the middle of the channel. It has a rare double barrier reef protecting it from ocean currents and waves. Shaped like a seahorse, it is off the northwest coast of Madagascar. Its southern end has two large coves, virtually unpopulated."

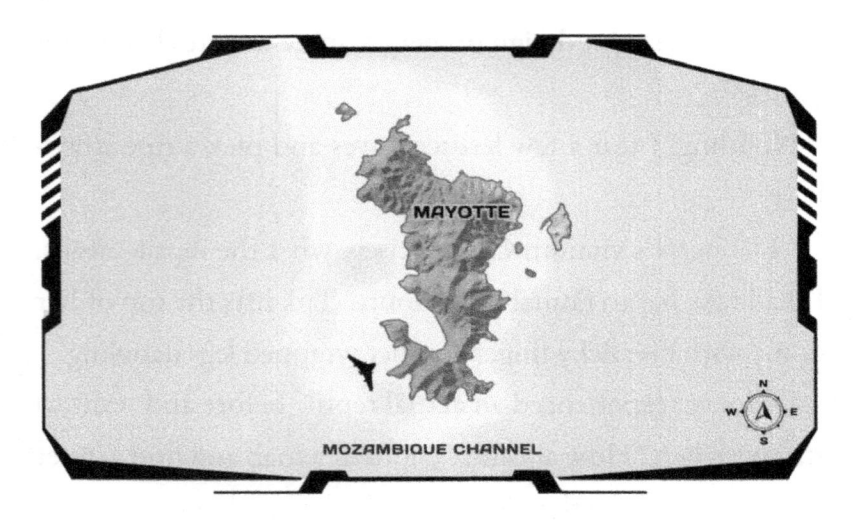

"In the seahorse's tail." Allia has finished the berry and I give her a scrap of lettuce. "And in the morning..."

"I shall locate White Wolf," Tuk finishes.

"I was going to say... tomorrow morning, after we feed everybody, we need to make your tattoo." I swallow hard. This won't be easy.

Cheerfully, Tuk agrees, "Yes!" and changes the subject, "Have you finished your latest song yet?"

I give him a hard look. He's never asked about my songs before. "Why do you ask?"

"Sing it for me? I would like to hear it." He nods.

All at once, I'm self-conscious. "Um...I don't think so."

"In that case, tell me about it? Perhaps I might read it?"

"It's about extinction."

"Of course, it is." He grins. "Send it to me before you go to sleep. I shall endeavor to get it to Nuwa."

Since when does *he* have access to Nuwa and why didn't he tell me before? "Seriously? You think you can?" Korave told me droids can lie, so I don't know if I believe him even for a nano.

"I shall try—for you and the millions of endangereds."

"I'll send it as soon as I tuck Allia in." Holding the tortoise, my sleeve inches up, exposing my fake, fading tattoo. I need to find a marker and redraw it. I want it there permanently.

16
Pangolins and the Wrong Tattoo

We divvy up the chores. Tuk makes lab food for Sleuth, Buzzie and Hogman, and at night, we clean Sleuth's, Hogman's and Buzzie's rooms together. That means we bring them, one by one, into the hall, while Tootega activates jets in the ceiling to dissolve the biodegradable bedding down the floor drains. Then Tootega adds fresh bedding. Tuk feeds Hogman while I feed Sleuth, Buzzie, Antoadia and Mig. The Slimendiggers? They love their rotting banana leaves.

Snacking on berries at the galley table, I watch Antoadia watching the Slimendiggers gunge their way around the leaves. Tuk's downstairs feeding Hogman. I helped him unwrap Allia's legs, then fed Sleuth. He's restless, no longer limping. Buzzie's stronger too. She hopped off the perch when I threw her a piece of lab meat.

Tuk appears in the galley doorway. "I just received Red Dragon news."

I sit up, and my breath quickens with dread.

"Tootega, pull up a map of Southeast Asia," Tuk asks.

The galley lightscreen shows a country that's bordered by China, Thailand and Bangladesh.

"Observe," Tuk says, "Myanmar experienced a brief period of democracy early in the century but has been unstable ever since. This has allowed all manner of nefarious poachers to find refuge there."

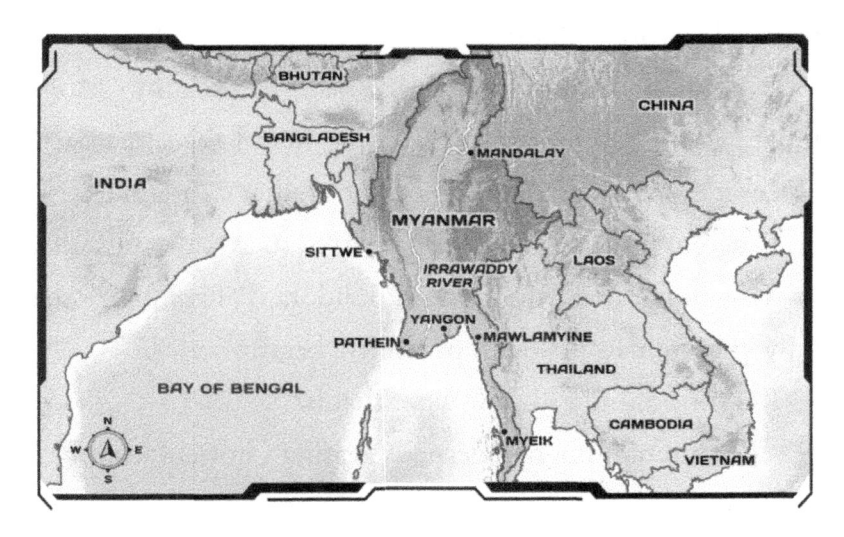

"Terrible," I reply, watching Antoadia stalk her breakfast cricket.

"Asian WEAPPs orchestrated a sting operation to catch as many of the gang as possible."

My mind flashes back... on Mom and Dad in their azure uniforms, in my doorway on that Saturday that feels like a hundred years ago. My eyes brim with tears.

"Yeah?" I reply, my voice choked.

"Zoom in to Myanmar, Tootega," Tuk says. "The country has an extensive coastline. Even accounting for the rise in sea level, it still has several major seaports where international ships deliver cargo of all kinds. Tootega, indicate ports."

Five lights blink along the coast.

"Red Dragons were caught smuggling the last Pangolins in the world, worth billions."

"Pangolins? Pangolins...*Pangolins*!" I exclaim. Mom must've said pangolins, but we only heard the olins part! "Does it even matter that I don't know what a Pangolin is?"

"Pangolins are mammals, also referred to as scaly anteaters, or trenggiling, from the Order Pholidota. Pangolins are the only known mammal with protective keratin scales."

"Keratin? Should I know what that is?"

"The stuff of human fingernails, feathers, horns and wool."

"Bizarre."

Tuk slides into the chair across from me. "Red Dragons captured these Pangolins in the Philippines. They no doubt intended to smuggle them through Myanmar to China and sell them to the highest bidder for some millionaires' dinner."

"Horrible..."

"However," Tuk holds up his finger, "two members evaded capture." He turns to face me. "White Wolf and his android henchman captured the largest shipment of Pangolins and were not caught.... *yet*," he adds slyly. "As we speak, they are cruising international waters aboard White Wolf's superyacht."

Tuk turns toward the lightscreen. "Tootega, display an image of the *Yanbu*."

A sleek, white ship appears with five decks, four lifeboats, and a helicopter on a landing pad.

"Behold," Tuk says with a wave at the screen, "White Wolf's superyacht."

"That's the biggest boat I've ever seen!"

"Tootega, display an image of White Wolf."

An ugly, thin man with long, white hair appears in red pajamas. He has a hooked nose, a huge jaw and a fat lower lip with a chin that sticks out. I gasp softly. It's the man from my dream! If he is real, does that mean my parents are being held prisoner too??? Maybe on that very yacht?

"White Wolf is known to disguise himself and regularly uses aliases. Charles Phillips, Joseph Franks, Phillip Peters, and Frank Joseph are a few of the names he uses. He is known as White Wolf because of his hair."

"He's so hideous and not at all what I imagined. I thought he'd be old, wrinkled and mean looking."

"Tootega, show us Big Bear," Tuk orders. "This is his android henchman, an XH5. Designed after sumo wrestlers, they are quite large. Still, for all their bulk, they possess a limited data base with an absurdly lethargic processing speed."

Big Bear's head grows nearly straight out of his immense chest.

"A total freak-a-droid!" I exclaim. "Like a sumo mated with a titanic toad."

"An appropriate assessment." Tuk stands. "White Wolf has his shipment of pangolins somewhere here," he indicates a spot on the map, "in the Bay of Bengal."

"These poor creatures have been the most heavily trafficked endangereds in this century, possibly linked to the corona virus pandemic in 2019."

I feel stupid and admit, "I've never heard of them."

"Many consider their flesh a delicacy. Peoples in certain Asian countries still believe traditional remedies with pangolin scales possess medicinal qualities, particularly for women who have trouble nursing their infants. What with poaching, trafficking and dwindling habitat, pangolins are critically endangered."

"If fingernails were medicine, everyone should bite their own and eat them!" I reply.

"True. Unfortunately for pangolins, keratin is not medicinal."

My mouth droops. "People are so *stupid*."

"I shall hack Big Bear's internal GPS to determine their location…" He pauses, his eyes brighten, and his pupils dilate. He blinks furiously, as if his eyelashes are having a seizure. He continues. "Once we pinpoint their location and make contact, we will arrange a meeting." He smiles, flashing his perfect teeth.

Why is he smiling? This is the most dangerous thing ever! Not something to smile about! A wall of alabaster cages flares in my mindsight. My thoughts race…will they believe we're gang members… what if they don't…even if they do, how do we save the pangolins…White Wolf and Big Bear must be armed. I wonder if I could overpower White Wolf. There's no way Tuk stands a chance against that gargantuan freak-a-droid. "And then what?" I ask.

"I would rather not share my plan until it is entirely formulated."

"Better formulate in a hurry." I glare and wipe my sweaty palms on my pants.

It's taken all morning at the galley table to trace the dragon's outline, face and scales with Tuk's smart pen. He's kept his eyes closed the whole time. In the fourth hour my hand cramps into a claw.

Initially I felt awkward touching his cool arm and chest. I wasn't sure if his hair or armpit had an odor, but being so close to him with his shirt off, I could smell him...like sparks from my fire starter. So weird!

Tracing the final scale, I announce, "Done!" I stand to stretch and massage my hand. The tattoo looks fantastic, if I say so myself. All it needs is color.

"I shall begin tinting the dragon and complete the process with an explosion of color." Tuk keeps his eyes closed when tones of gray instantly begin to shade the beast. From light to dark, the writhing tail blossoms, wrapping around his forearm. Then the body, legs and head climb around his bicep. Rising like a wave, the dragon comes to life, curling, rolling, and coiling over his shoulder. Faint tones appear in its fangs, tongue and furious face that angles up his pectoral muscle giving the dragon depth and dimension. Color comes at the end, blooming in an instant. ALL WRONG! It's not red, it's GREEN! *A bright green dragon!*

"Are you color blind?! The dragon is supposed to be *RED*! They're called Red Dragons! Not Green Dragons!!!" I'm yelling but I can't help myself. This is a disaster.

He stares at his arm and chest. Frowning he says, "System error!" as if he were cursing.

"So, change the color! That should be easy for an XH7! Come on!"

He shakes his head. "Once I alter my smartskin, my system requires a complete restore. That means returning to my default appearance, which means starting over again."

I refuse to accept this. "System restores are easy. I've rebooted my miniQ and maxiQ a million times. *Just do it!*"

Staring at his bicep, he moans, "I am an exceedingly complex system, Luki, with subsystems containing dozens of subsystems. A complete restore requires that I am incapacitated for seventy-two hours, and we cannot afford to wait that long. Furthermore, I am stupefied that *my* system should cause such an absurd error more common for inferior XH models." Forlorn, he shakes his head with contempt.

Whenever I compare myself to somebody in virtual school who's smarter, or who has lots of actual friends, or the latest VR gear, Aana tells me, "Comparing yourself to others never serves you. You are unique with many talents. The gifts you are born with will take you far. You get nowhere trying to be someone else." Then Taata chimes in: 'You got to row with your own oars. Nobody else's.'

We don't have a choice. We must row with Tuk's grassy, green oars. We *must* use this tattoo. It's the only one we've got. "So why not be a member of the Green Dragon gang instead?" I shrug, his fire starter odor smells a lot stronger now.

Tuk's eyes flare. "What a tremendous idea! But not just any member—I am Chief Tuttuk, boss of the Green Dragons!" He growls, then flexes his biceps and looks more like a cocky teenage show-off than the commander of an international trafficking gang. But it would have to do.

17
Phishing on the Road to Mandalay

Night envelops the ship anchored in a cove off Rutland Island. It's one of the Andaman Islands in the Bay of Bengal.

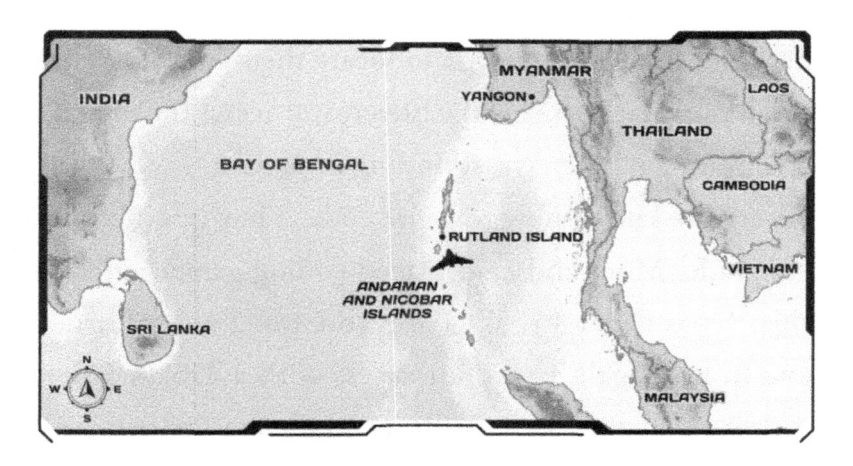

We're sitting in Mom and Dad's cabin, at the foot of their bed. The room glows from the three different lightscreens that fill the wall. He's been at it for hours. I don't know why, but it's taking him way too long to hack the freak-a-droid, Big Bear.

I close my eyes. White Wolf's superyacht is tangled and glowing with hundreds of slender spiritcords in my mind-sight. But where? After cruising all day, we still couldn't locate the colossal vessel.

"You made it sound like hacking his system was easy." I grab a pillow and flop on the bed.

Tuk's typing madly at the lightboard in his lap, his neck bent at an unnatural angle. "Every XH has built-in GPS."

I could fall asleep staring at the screens filled with code.

Tuk types faster than anyone, including Korave. Like millipede legs, his fingers ripple across the lightboard. "If the XH Corporation wants to locate their androids, they search their data base for the buyer, and access the model's serial number." He says, sounding impatient.

Everyone knows how to write code. They teach kids in first grade. Mom and Dad played coding games with me when I was three. I took classes too, but I never learned how to hack, gain backdoor access with a Trojan Horse or write a virus, like kids do all the time for fun, and sometimes money.

"I am attempting to use enumeration and access super-user privileges to hack the XH data base," Tuk mutters, "and for reasons I cannot explain, it is taking far longer than I expected. Nevertheless, I am confident I shall gain access to Big Bear's serial number." He moves to the middle of the bed, to the next lightscreen.

"It seems like you're making this really complicated." I yawn.

"This is demanding... and I do not recall soliciting your opinion..." His fingers continue their crazy millipede dance on the lightboard. "If my smartskin had the ability to perspire, I would be sweating..." He pauses a nano and squints out the porthole into the night, "...like a Belgian draft horse!"

"You're going around their firewall, or turning it off, right?" My knowledge was basic, but at least I knew *something*.

"Of course, I considered their firewall. Unlike homo sapiens, I am not programmed for forgetfulness...although that is an interesting consideration."

That's a *scary* consideration. "Droids should never be programmed to forget! That would be dangerous."

"With a bit of memory loss now and then, androids might become considerably more human... did I remember the firewall?" He slaps his forehead hard. "Oops, I forgot the firewall!"

Reaching over, I grab his arm. "Don't! You might damage your neural network, or neuromorphic chips!"

He jerks his arm away.

"How interesting...it is oddly satisfying to say, 'I forgot'...and my forehead slap?" He bonks his head with the heel of his palm again. "A bit of percussive stimulation does wonders, although you are correct to admonish me. If I hit too hard, I may well go into sleep mode, dislodge a neural component, or worse, risk harming my mindfile." He pounds his forehead again.

"So, STOP IT already!" I grab his arm again.

Droids with damaged mindfiles were Korave's hobby droids—the ones with shattered neural networks, the ones whose heads took a beating, like if they were smashed in a hovercycle accident. Korave said you could always tell when a droid had damage to their affective computing module. They might lose their ability to emote and develop a repetitive behavior, like Tourette's Syndrome. With moderate damage they might curse and be disagreeable with weird tics. The ones with serious damage exhibit a behavior called Phineas Gage Syndrome. They become raving psycho-criminals and might even self-destruct. *Robocide*. Korave says it used to be rare but happens more and more these days.

"As for their firewall, I am using a virtual private network redirecting my network to a foreign country. I am being channeled through Iceland as we speak."

"Does XH have a MEMYSELFi page?" Almost everyone has one—except me. I'm not allowed until I'm fifteen. I wanted one before... but who cares anymore? I don't.

"Naturally," he declares without looking up. "The XH page features every model the company produces. It encourages customers to post videos of their androids doing fantastic things, as well as ridiculous, degrading and demeaning activities, which most customers prefer posting."

"You're programmed with the company's email address, right?"

"Of course. Every model has it in their database," he replies staring at the lightscreen.

"Give me the lightboard a nano." I flip onto my back with my knees bent and my boots on the bed. Mom would kill me for this.

He passes it over and I balance it on my knees.

"I'm going to phish for the company password—on their MEMYSELFi page." It's preposterously basic, but worth a try because it's the one and only hack I know. I'm sure he's going to tell me I'm being naive... that it's way too simple... that nobody ever uses a password for more than one site.

With a look of surprise, he admits, "I had not considered that."

"Okay...I'm writing that I've just posted a video of you on their MEMYSELFi page—something thoroughly humiliating, like...I modified you...to...perform like a Ssanibot." I snicker. "Now I'm directing the administrator to click the link to watch you lick the floor and—"

"The administrator clicks the link..." he nods, seeing where this is going.

"I lead them to a log-in page, they enter their password... we wait a few seconds.... and...." I gasp in disbelief, "I've got them!" Stunned, I pass the lightboard to him and flop onto my belly.

His fingers speed across the lightboard with rapid clicks, taps and pings and in seconds, he's got Big Bear's serial number and the exact location of White Wolf's superyacht.

"Tootega, pull up a map of the Bay of Bengal on lightscreen one," Tuk orders.

The codes dissolve and a large map appears.

"Tootega, indicate the following position: 15.788675 latitude, 94.287085 longitude."

A blinking crimson dot appears. The yacht isn't in the Bay of Bengal, after all! It's near the delta of Burma's largest river, in the Andaman Sea.

"Tootega, enlarge."

I sit up, rub my burning eyes, and study the map. "Know what I think?"

"I am not programmed to be a mind reader."

Rolling off the bed, I stick my finger in the lightscreen. "This river runs through the entire country. If I were trafficking endangereds, I wouldn't unload at a port along the coast. Way too dangerous. White Wolf knows WEAPP is on high alert. I'd cruise up this river, the... Irra... waddy instead."

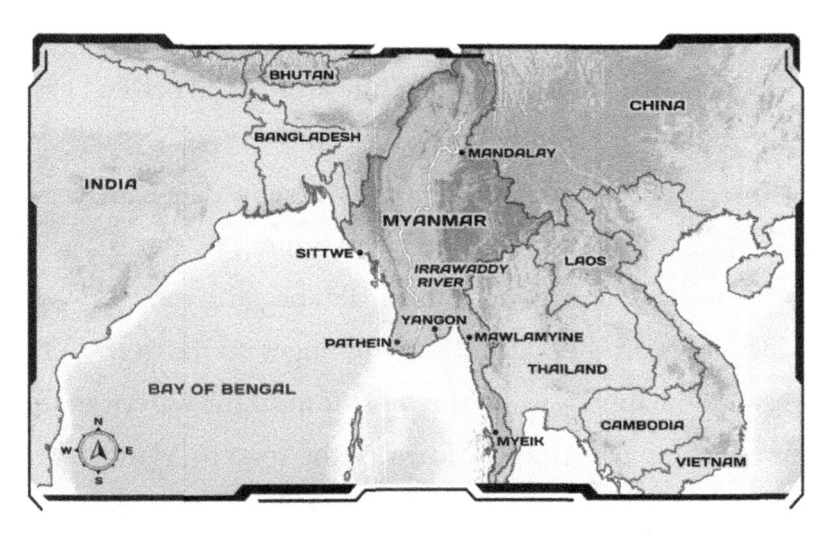

"And take the road to Mandalay!" Tuk replies, suddenly bright and cheery.

"Huh?... what are you talking about? He's in a boat."

He turns, grabs my shoulder, and with a strange accent announces, *"Come you back to Mandalay, Where the old Flotil-*

la lay: *Can't you 'ear their paddles chunkin' from Rangoon to Mandalay? On the road to Mandalay, Where the flyin'-fishes play, An' the dawn comes up like thunder outer China 'crost the Bay...!"*

I stare at him like a chip in his neural network might've slipped. "What *are you talking about?!*" I'm too tired for Tuk's games.

"You must know Rudyard Kipling's poem, *Road to Mandalay*. He only wrote one of your favorite stories—*The Jungle Book*."

"What's that got to do with White Wolf? And before I pass out, would you please tell me your plan!"

"It seems I cannot control myself when my data bank cross references!" Tuk smiles, tickled with himself.

"So, tell me." I clasp my hands. "I'm begging you!"

He jumps off the bed and runs his finger up the river. "The Irrawaddy happens to be the most important waterway for commerce in Myanmar, known as the road to Mandalay. I believe your instincts are correct, that White Wolf plans to take his pangolins up the Irrawaddy to Mandalay here," he points to a city in the north, his finger on the word, Mandalay. "If I were White Wolf, that is precisely where I would unload my illicit cargo, in the city of my headquarters and that much closer to China."

"So...we're going to follow them up the river to Mandalay and notify WEAPP and INTERPOL before we get there?"

"Let us discuss this in the morning, when we are nearer the superyacht, and you are well rested. I commend your instincts, Luki. Well done!" He pats me on the back.

"That sounds like yes," I mutter as I stomp off to my cabin.

18
All We Have is Each Other

I've fed everyone their breakfast and stare out the galley window at the turquoise water when Tuk appears behind me.

"Time to contact Big Bear!" He grins and heads to the cockpit.

I don't even have time to get nervous. By the time I get to the cockpit, he's already making the call—and he still hasn't told me his plan, even if he *has* one. It sounds like he's talking to a little kid. I peer over his shoulder. The freak-a-droid's face fills the lightscreen.

He may look like a Sumo wrestler, but he sounds like a four-year-old. "What is your organization?" His vocal circuitry must've been damaged in an accident...or a fight? His absurdly high-pitched voice doesn't match his size—at all.

"We are the Green Dragons." Tuk lifts his sleeve and turns his tattooed arm toward the screen.

"Never heard of you." Big Bear squints, shaking his head.

"We are new to the business and come with a collection of healthy samples your chief executive will find of great interest."

Big Bear lurches when he glimpses me behind Tuk. "Who is that?" He points a fat, sausage-like finger.

Tuk shifts in the chair, pulling me over his shoulder, "This is my assistant, Luki"

"Unusual...attractive," Big Bear peeps.

I don't like the way the freak-a-droid looks, sounds or peeps at me.

Tuk wastes no time getting to the point. "Is it possible to show our samples in a virtual meeting, and then meet live?"

I've got to admire his confidence.

"Nothing virtual. Everything live. All business conducted on the *Yanbu*," the freak-a-droid squeaks.

"In that case, we shall bring our samples with us." Tuk looks at me and winks. "That is not a problem."

Butterflies do flips in my stomach. That's a *terrible* idea!

Big Bear raises a sausage finger. "Wait. I must request this meeting with the chief."

He exits the screen, his grotesque feet flapping across a milky white floor. Why is he barefoot? Then it hits me. *He was in my dream!* Mom and Dad *must* be alive, prisoners on that yacht! The possibility makes we want to jump and shout.

Tuk mutes the screen and turns to me. "This is going so well. Do you agree?" He seems a little too cocky to me.

"You still haven't told me your plan!" I snap, more nervous by the nano.

"Trust me." Tuk juts his jaw.

My lips tighten. "I trust your mindfile and your data base. But landing *Anniqsuqti* on the *Yanbu* puts us in serious jeopardy."

"How very contrary!" He scowls as Big Bear approaches. Tuk turns back to the lightscreen and unmutes.

"Chief says okay with one condition," he raises the sausage finger. "No miniature quantum computers allowed."

No miniQ's?! My heart races. That means no access...to WEAPP...to INTERPOL...to Aana, Taata...to Korave! We're *doomed* if something happens! I will never listen to a droid again!

"Fine," Tuk agrees without protest.

"What is your transport?" Big Bear squeaks.

"A Falcon AEV."

"I will transmit the *Yanbu's* landing coordinates. How soon should I expect you?" The freak-a-droid asks.

"Give us forty-five minutes." Tuk grins.

"I will be waiting." Big Bear nods as the lightscreen goes black.

"Excellent!" Tuk smiles, rubbing his palms together.

"Will you please stop having so much fun! You're supposed to be serious. Levelheaded! We're on high alert! And we're not even allowed one miniQ? This is *insanely dangerous!* You realize that don't you?!"

His eyes narrow, and his pupils shrink to pinheads. "Luki... I am thrilled that we shall soon apprehend the largest animal trafficker in the world, although, according to my data base, there is nothing White Wolf does not traffic in." He gives my arm a firm pat. "Try not to be so apprehensive, will you?"

"But what if something horrible happens?" I whine, wondering why I ever went along with him in the first place, dreading that something horrible *will* happen.

"What can I tell you?" He shrugs. "I am hard-wired for calm. Besides, our chances for success are based on the principle of improbability and its five laws."

I roll my eyes and Tuk starts counting on his fingers. "There is the Law of Inevitability, the Law of Truly Large Numbers, the Law of Selection, the Law of the Probability Lever and the Law of Near Enough."

"I've never heard of any of them!" I protest, wondering if he's making it up? "Principle of what? Law of Near Enough?" If he weren't a droid, I'd swear he was full of walrus blubber.

"That law proves anyone is psychic."

"Those laws are so obscure!" I'm irritated, shouting. "And of any law, it's the one I should know, but I've *never ever* heard of it! What's your point, anyway?!"

"My objective is to make you understand that we are powerful together. You have me... and I have you..." He continues with a twirl of his finger, "... and we have them," he says, referring to the animals downstairs, "and they.... have us. Collectively, the logical outcome...is our triumph."

That's how the most sophisticated droid on earth describes our bond? The one that unites humans, animals and AI—like a three-year-old? I sigh heavily. But I guess he's right. All we have is each other.

He flings out his arms. "As a group, we cannot fail. We shall accomplish this!"

"I still don't know your plan." I say for the thousandth time with quiet frustration.

He heads down the hall ignoring me and tosses over his shoulder, "I believe it is best that you remain...uninformed."

I'm so frustrated, I could explode when an idea pops into my head. I will find the tiniest miniQ and wrap it around Allia's neck, hidden under her scute, the one above her head that flares. No one will know it's there. Not even Tuk.

19

Salesman on a Ship from an Octopus's Dream

We're in hover mode. "That's it, isn't it?" I ask, pointing at the yacht half a mile away on the eastern horizon.

"Exquisite, is she not?" Tuk asks.

Retrieving the binocs from the cockpit, I return to my spot at the galley table and gaze at the gleaming yacht. "I've never seen anything like her."

"Four hundred feet long and five decks tall."

"She's beautiful...like...I can't even describe it..."

"A hydrodynamic coral reef?" Tuk suggests.

"Yeah ... and... and..."

"A bleached and buoyant sub-aquatic ecosystem, flawlessly symmetrical?" He asks.

"Yea... like a ship from an octopus's dream," I reply. I lay the binocs on the table and rub my sweaty palms on the seat of my pants. "Let's discuss what happens after we touch down on the *Yanbu's* helicopter pad."

"First, I shall inquire of Big Bear about the *Yanbu* protocols. I am reasonably certain they will not want us to haul our samples off *Anniqsuqti*. After we land aboard the *Yanbu*, White Wolf will board our ship for the presentation of our endangereds. As soon as he boards, you will direct Tootega to retract the stairs or cargo ramp and lock both egresses. I will then contact WEAPP and INTERPOL. Mission accomplished." He smiles. "Apprehending White Wolf will be child's play."

I start to panic as I listen. His idea is preposterous. Moronic even. "Not even for a nano are you considering the possibility that they're going to want us to unload our endangereds onto their ship. What then? Huh?" I head to storage for Dad's Xip3, his jacket with the built-in backpack. I don't know why, but I sense I'm going to need it.

Big Bear waits on the deck of the superyacht below the landing pad. Turns out they want our endangereds in their cages on the *Yanbu!* But the narrow landing pad won't allow our cargo ramp to open. We've got to use the narrow, exterior stairs, and there's no way we can get Hogman down those, which isn't a bad thing.

Tuk's so excited, he can't wait to get off *Anniqsuqti* and descends the stairs to the *Yanbu* deck with Buzzie squawking the whole way. The vulture is tethered to his wrist using Dad's eagle gauntlet. Before I get Allia, Mig, and Antoadia, and before I step outside, I pull Dad's jacket off. Something heavy is poking me in the back, something he left in the pack. Opening the pack, I find the bola I made for him with his favorite beach stones. It may be a primitive, but at least it's *something*. I roll the braided lines around the stones, put the jacket on and stuff the bola in my pocket. I put Mig on a leash, stuff Antoadia in the mesh outer pocket, and grab Allia. Outside, the heat is stifling. Clutching the tortoise to my stomach I hold my breath. Mig pulls. He's not used to a leash. My legs feel like jelly.

Big Bear points across the deck to a set of glass doors. "Cage your samples in the saloon below," he squeaks, directing us to a swooping staircase.

He stands with his swiveling robotically, tracking our movement.

Big Bear is huge, maybe six and half feet tall with a massive upper body. His neck-less head sits between his shoulders, like a fat carbuncle. He wears a tight black t-shirt, his elephantine biceps straining the fabric of the sleeves. Black skintight breeches taper to his ankles. His gargantuan thighs are like tree trunks and his feet are flat and wide as flippers.

The endangereds all sense a threat. Buzzie squawks and Antoadia leaks urine as I place her in a cage near Allia.

"*Out, out, OUT,*" Mig growls loudest of all.

Tuk heads back to the ship and returns with Sleuth who twitters, sending his mind pictures of hunters, "*Bad, danger, trouble, pain,*" he chirps in my mind's ear.

Like me, they know the *Yanbu* isn't safe. Tuk on the other hand, appears perfectly calm and unflappable, exactly as programmed.

I'm almost blinded by the sun in the all-white saloon. The room is vast and empty, except for the cages and two pale couches with white coffee tables that seem to float, like fossilized belugas on a frozen sea.

Tuk latches Sleuth's cage and turns to the freak-a-droid who's followed us down.

Tuk glances at me with a wink and announces, "Behold, our samples."

Like sentinels, we stand at either end of the wall of cages, the animals between us.

Big Bear approaches Tuk, and like one gorilla grooming the other, the freak-a-droid inspects Tuk's wrists, neck, pockets, even his ears for a miniQ. He flaps over to me and I get the same scrutiny. He pulls the bola from my pocket.

"What is this?" He asks.

"Just a game," I reply with as much indifference as I can muster.

"Show me." He squeaks and gives it back.

I start a stone going in one direction, and pumping my hand up and down, start the other stone going in the opposite direction. Big Bear's head bobs up and down, watching.

"Centripetal force powers the stones." Tuk says.

I add, "It's called Eskimo orbit."

"Keep your stupid game." Big Bear says. "Remain here. I get the chief."

Big Bear turns, the soles of his feet slapping across the floor, and vanishes down another stairway. Relieved, I take a deep breath, stop pumping my hand and the stones drop. I roll the bola up and stuff it in pocket. Staring at the floor, my mindsight flashes on Mom and Dad, pale, tired, frazzled, their clothes wrinkled, hair a mess, scared. Maybe sick? Pulsating silver threads flare in my mindsight—hundreds of fine, glowing strands twist through the floor, and crawl up the walls with a soft shaking sound, like a rattlesnake's tail. Pangolins!

"Good afternoon," a voice not much louder than a whisper greets us. A slender man with long white hair appears dressed in traditional Chinese clothing—red silk pants and jacket, like pajamas—*just like my dream!* His face is pale, taut and shiny with indifferent blue eyes. His hooked nose and chin look even bigger in person. He clutches a baby pangolin rolled in a ball in his pasty fingers and pokes at her with a baby bottle full of milk. Her cloud of fear engulfs him.

In a soft foreign accent, he asks, "Please...show me your samples," and sinks onto the nearest couch. Again and again, without even looking, he pokes the pangolin with the bottle trying to get her to uncurl. She refuses.

Tuk unlocks Sleuth's cage, hooks the leash around his collar, and walks the painted dog back and forth between the couches. Sleuth springs nervously, while Tuk gives his sales pitch.

"It is our great fortune to access a steady supply of the extremely desirable, critically endangered African wild dog, a species that teeters on the precipice of extinction. Known for its unique markings, the wild dog's hide makes an ideal area rug for..." he pauses, and looks up, his eyelashes flickering at the ceiling, "... a bathroom or before the fireplace!"

Expressionless, White Wolf listens, the baby bottle forgotten for the moment.

"The large round ears of the magnificent cape hunting dog make beautiful bowls, and its legs make stylish supports for tables. The texture and taste of its flesh, similar to the scarce hyena *and,*" he pauses, leaning into the gross, waxen man, "nutritionally, this dog's liver contains an abundance of minerals and B vitamins. Perhaps greatest of all—an elixir concocted from its feces cures hiccups and flatulence."

That sounds horrible and laughable and totally untrue... unless his neural network is being persuasive and untruthful.... I sure hope it's not true!

"Next one," White Wolf says, his mouth barely moving and mumbles something to Big Bear who stands behind the couch.

Big Bear leans in. The ugly man drops the pangolin and bottle in the freak-a-droid's cupped hands. Like trying to pry a stubborn lid off a jar, he turns it this way and that, but the frightened Pangolin remains in its protective ball.

Returning Sleuth to the cage, Tuk pulls on the gauntlet and reaches for Buzzie. She squawks loudly as she nears the grotesque man.

"Virtually every part of this charismatic bird has the potential to be utilized." Tuk sits on the edge of the table and extends the gauntlet toward White Wolf's face. "Due to their immense size, these birds possess more succulent feet-meat than chicken, duck or even ostrich! Boiled, then sauteed, their talons are delicious with garlic, sesame oil and a dash of oyster sauce." Tuk licks his lips.

I watch fascinated. Tuk has transformed himself into a smarmy salesman, grotesque but impressive.

"Like the vultures', the wild dog's liver has an abundance of iron and B vitamins. Perhaps due to their unusual diet, the avian flesh is an excellent immune booster. With the recent outbreak of bubonic plague, a mere one hundred grams prevents pestilence in the adult human for up to one full year. That is, in addition to warding off the common cold and influenza." Tuk gently pulls one of Buzzie's wings. "And discriminating fashionistas demand these beautiful smoky feathers."

"Nice." White Wolf nods, massaging his cheeks and forehead, stretching the skin on his face. "What else?"

Tuk returns Buzzie to her cage and retrieves Allia, still retracted, and sets her on the table near White Wolf's knees where she remains clammed up in her shell.

"Arguably the most beautiful, critically endangered reptile is the radiated tortoise, which foodies believe is best in soup, though I prefer its silky, melt-in-your-mouth flesh poached in butter with pepper, Persian blue salt and lemon zest on a bed of quinoa." Tuk smacks his lips.

The repulsive man's eyes dart from Tuk to Allia and back again.

"Its carapace makes an exquisite bowl for fruit, candy, pot pourri...and used as a shade, creates an exotic lighting effect." Scooping her up, he places her against the wall, near the cages. "A light source added to the interior of the carapace adds drama to any living space." Placing her back on the table, he leans and whispers. "Unequaled among reptilian endangereds, the female's eggs increase a woman's fruitfulness, critical these days with Asia's moribund fertility rates. With a steady supply from our members in Madagascar, Green Dragons can guarantee gravid females for a premium price."

"The market is excellent for the beautiful reptile," says White Wolf, his mouth lifting in a creepy half smile as he massages his neck and chin.

Meanwhile, the freak-a-droid behind the couch still prods the scaly baby, unable to make her uncurl.

Tuk returns Allia to her cage and grabs Antoadia claiming she tastes better than frog and that her skin "cures a variety of dermatologic complaints." He declares, "When the bony plate in her head is dehydrated, ground into a powder and snorted, it effectively enhances vital energies for men."

He rhapsodizes about Mig's heart, liver and kidneys. "Rare delicacies loaded with vitamins... their tails and skins are most desirable as coats in select northern markets. However, best of all," he exclaims, "whether boiled, sauteed, pickled or dehydrated, arctic fox eyes promote night vision!"

Catching my breath, my mouth droops. So far I've listened to his horrible descriptions without reacting, but this is too much.

After caging Mig, Tuk sits on the couch across from White Wolf. "Are you looking for something specific? Whatever it is, I trust we can assist you."

"All your samples are nice...." He leers—his teeth a disgusting yellow. "Did you bring any more?"

"I can generate a hologram of the magnificent Mangalitsa, representative of a healthy supply, but due to his robust size, bringing him on board is not feasible. You are familiar with the pig's richly marbled flesh, so creamy it literally melts in the mouth?"

Stone-faced, White Wolf shakes his head, "The Mangalitsa is not endangered. What else have you got?"

"The critically endangered Partula island snail," Tuk says, "but they are still..."

White Wolf cuts him off. "Show me. The market is enormous for endangered snails." He turns, glancing at Big Bear, who's given up feeding the baby.

"The snails are on our ship," Tuk raises a finger. "Just one quick minute." He jumps from the couch, jogs across the room, and bounds up the stairs.

If Tuk were sentient and conscious, he could hear my telepathic scream, *"DON'T LEAVE ME ALONE WITH THESE MONSTERS!"*

The repulsive man murmurs to the freak-a-droid who nods, dropping the pangolin and the bottle in White Wolf's lap. The freak-a-droid trails Tuk and flaps across the room and up the stairs. My heart starts pounding so loud I'm sure White Wolf can hear it. I grin nervously at him, and start counting the seconds until Tuk returns.

20
The Baby Needs Milk

Gesturing with the bottle, he beckons me, "Why don't you try. The baby needs milk."

I don't want to get anywhere near him, but need to do what he says... what choice do I have? I inch over to the couch and sit on the edge. He passes the scaly baby and bottle to me and spreads his arms wide on the back of the couch, watching me. I want to soothe this terrified creature, but the way I feel—I need soothing myself! I take a deep breath and try to relax. Moments pass. I focus on her, calming myself a little. She's so sweet and small nestled in my lap.

I feel her moving, opening, coming to life. Scale-by-scale she unfurls in my hands, blooming in slow motion, like a bronze flower. Almost eight inches long, her bright eyes shine like tiny black beads and her pink nose glistens at the end of her snout. She snorts at my arms and face, like a dainty sneeze as I place the bottle under her nose. Hungrily, she latches on and pulls hard, her pointy little claws pressing into my hand. I trace the graceful curve of her ridged ear with my finger and marvel at her strangeness. She's like a mini dinosaur, or an alien from another planet. She's perfect, extraordinary, sweet, innocent and *bizarre*, and her contentment is the only thing I feel. I'm so focused, for a nano I forget where I am, but suddenly I feel something crawl up my back and freeze. I whip my head around. *His hand!!!*

The foul wolf touches my braid. "Beautiful," he whispers, like I'm some endangered species he wants to add to his collection.

Adrenalin surges through me. Clutching the baby, I pull away and she rolls into a ball.

"DO NOT TOUCH ME!" I shriek, eyes wide. All at once, I'm so angry I could kill. My mindsight screams, *'WHERE ARE YOU, TUK?!'*

White Wolf pats the couch. "I promise. No touching," he whispers. "Come sit by me."

Trembling with rage and disgust, I blurt, "I'll stand until Tuk's back!"

The misshapen man nods with his disgusting yellow teeth smile. My heart pounds...my thoughts race wildly... what is taking Tuk so long?... what happened to Big Bear...? WHERE is Tuk...? I will never believe another droid again. What's so special about *this* pangolin...? Why does he want to feed it...? What is he going to do with me...? Where is Tuk?

We're going to be killed... No.... I'm going to be killed, Tuk's just a droid... he can't die.... and why this pangolin?!

He's watching me... watching my face... watching my eyes dart around the room while my thoughts bubble up like methane through permafrost.

"You have a question?" He asks.

As if he cares! Don't want to talk...don't want to say anything to this evil snake...not another word... but... need to know... feel like crying... want to beg him not to kill me, and blurt, "Why are you feeding this baby?!"

His eyes brighten. "To fatten up for dinner, of course and you can join me." He smiles and runs his tongue over his lips.

I stifle a gasp as Big Bear thumps down the stairs, crosses the room and nods to the ugly snake. The snake rises, straightens his jacket and barks orders for the ships' navigation in a foreign language. German? I recognize one word, *Mandalay*. The engines rev higher. In seconds, we pick up speed, heading, I guess, straight for the mouth of the Irrawaddy River.

"Where is Tuk?!" My words are clipped with fury.

White Wolf approaches. "The baby likes you," he declares, as she unrolls for me. "Who is this duck?"

"Mr. Tuttuk!" I nearly shriek.

"He waits upstairs to discuss business, where I go now. Feed the baby. Make him fat and juicy." He shoots Big Bear a look.

The freak-a-droid nods and like a ghostly devil, White Wolf glides across the room and up the stairs.

Big Bear flaps over and stands inches away from me. Without a word, he lifts me up and carries me to the cages. Instantly I sense they know we're impostors and the whole thing has been a masquerade.

"STOP! STOP IT! PUT ME DOWN!" I shout, punching with the hand gripping the bottle, clutching the pangolin in the other. Waving her tail back and forth, she sounds like a rattlesnake. It's useless to resist. Punching the freak-a-droid hasn't done anything except squirt milk down his back!

He puts me in a cage at the far end, bolts the door and heads upstairs. I'm alone, imprisoned behind bars in this barren room… Tuk's missing and there's no way to reach him.

The baby stops rattling. She wants to feed again, but the milk's almost gone because I wasted it. My mind races to Mig and the endangereds… are they going to be sold… killed, skinned and eaten? Will they become bowls, lights, coats, rugs, table legs? What's going to happen to me? Will I become the ugly creep's slave? Will he sell me to the highest bidder? But I'm just a kid and kids like to pretend, and I've pretended that I knew what I was doing and we were doing something important and would find Mom and Dad, but I don't know anything anymore. It's hopeless and horrifying and I can't stop thinking horrible thoughts, and I'm breathing too fast, in the grip of panic... dizzy... lightheaded.... everything colorless, bleached. I lower my head between my knees and exhale .... count to four. Inhale.... count to four. I'm sinking... falling into a black hole. So much for Tuk's plan. Inhale. Exhale. Sip the air. Mig yips. Wants out. They all want out. I want out.

I dig into my pocket, wrap my fingers around a stone and squeeze hard. It's cold but feels good in my hand. I will use it to cripple that horrible, ugly, snake of a man. It won't be difficult. All I need is one moment...two or three nanos.... that's all it will take. One good swing above my head, aim at his legs and release. He needs to be far enough away, at least twenty feet. I know I can do it, but will I have the chance? A burst of confidence shoots through me.

"Kalluk," Mom's favorite Inupiaq curse pops into my head. Staring through the bars, I mutter "Kalluk." I say it again, louder, "Kalluk!" My mindsight flashes on hundreds of glowing spiritcords, like bright silver threads that tangle up through the floor. A rage I've never felt overwhelms me like a wave. I scream, *"KALLUK!"* and kick the gate with such force, two of the bars actually bend! The baby rolls up into a ball again. It feels great to kick! Again, and again...and again I kick the bars that bend with each blow. I keep kicking until there's a hole large enough to wriggle through.

Before crawling out, I zip the baby into the back of Dad's jacket and a voice whispers something. What? Sandy wind swirls across a desert. I hear it again. It's the tortoise. I squirm through the bars and try to stand but wobble. Something's wrong with my bionic foot. *Can't* care—not now. Allia is trying to tell me something! *What?*

Allia sends a picture of Tuk. Her sultry, sandy voice says, "*Machine man is okay.*"

"What? Where is he?!" I ask with a picture of Tuk holding her in the galley.

I take a step and crumple to the floor. I lift my leg and try pointing my bionic toes but my entire foot flips back. The broken ankle dangles like a freakish double joint. I can't put weight on it. I get up carefully, putting all the weight on my good foot, bend my knee to steady myself, and let the bionic foot hang.

Allia sends a picture of Tuk in a waterfall. "*He's in the monsoon.*" Her deep voice swirls with sand.

Waterfall? Monsoon? Where? The only water is the sea.

Like Antoadia, I hop-limp to the giant glass door and slide it open and limp onto a narrow balcony to peer over the railing and... there! Clinging to the side of the ship, at water level is Tuk!

Water washes over him as we churn through the delta. Tuk lifts one arm, pushing his palm flat, then the opposite foot, then his other arm—pressing his fingers, palms and toes against the ship's slick surface, trying to climb, trying to get traction. He keeps sliding down. I wave at him. He sees me. His lips move, trying to tell me something I can't hear above the engines drone. I hop-limp back to Allia's cage, take her out and slip her inside the jacket, against my belly for warmth. She's *got* to emerge! Exhaling my hot breath down inside the jacket for extra warmth, her head and neck slowly appear.

Whispering, "Thank you, Allia!" I unbuckle the miniQ and slip it around my thumb. As she retracts in the frigid air, I put her back in the cage. Hobbling outside, I whisper-yell, "Tuk!" into the miniature device. "They're onto us! The freak-a-droid caged me, but I kicked my way out and busted my foot. We've got to get them!"

"Pangolins.... hundreds... alive!" he exclaims, scuttling up the ship and sliding down. The setae on his palms and feet must be too wet, and the vertical wall of the yacht is as slippery as ice.

"Climb above the waterline!" I yell. He scuttles up and slides back down. Scuttle and slide, until one hand finds a dry spot and sticks. Up goes his right hand and his left foot, then his left hand and right foot. Hand over hand, he scrambles up the wall going faster, like a wind-up toy, until he jumps over the deck railing and careens into the saloon.

"We must find Big Bear and White Wolf!" he says in a puddle of sea water forming at his feet.

"Give me a nano." Closing my eyes to focus my mindsight, I see them clearly. "They're... up on the bridge, in the bow." My body starts to tremble anticipating a confrontation.

When I open my eyes, Tuk is bent over running his hands down his legs, squeezing water from his pants.

As the puddle spreads, Mig, Sleuth, Buzzie, Allia and Antoadia clamor for freedom.

"*Out! Out! Out!*" Mig whines, sending pictures of the tundra.

Sleuth needs to run with a picture of the grassy savanna.

Frowning, Tuk points at Sleuth and talks so fast I can hardly make out what he's saying. "Our cape hunting dog there... his bite force quotient is the highest of any predator in the order Carnivora, which includes lions, tigers and bears."

"Slow down! What difference does his bite force make *NOW?*"

"We need that inferior android permanently disabled, which makes the wild dog ideal for the job!"

I don't need further convincing. "Fine!"

Tuk's babbling like Dad after too much coffee. "I estimate White Wolf's weight at 139 pounds. Light enough. ..." he pauses, his pupils dilating.

"For what?"

"For the vulture's talons to clutch his pallid flesh and drop him into the sea!" He pulls off his shirt and wrings it out on the floor.

He's so wrong. "Buzzie can't lift over thirty-five pounds. The strength of her talons does not correspond to her size, which must be in your data base *somewhere!*"

"*Fly,*" Buzzie screeches with an aerial picture of an evergreen forest.

"*Free us from this... pale purgatory,*" Allia moans with an image of a thorny thicket.

Tuk unrolls his shirt and swings it over his head, spraying me with salty drops. "How curious...my vision to drop White Wolf into the sea overrode my neuromorphic chips regarding the vulture's data. That has *never* happened before. In that case, I shall disable White Wolf myself, which should require little effort, given my strength and his slender physique. Afterwards, we shall take control of the ship and notify WEAPP and INTERPOL, who shall await our arrival in Mandalay."

Tuk is thinking *way* too logically. "Didn't that freak-a-droid just throw you overboard, like maybe... an hour ago?"

He stops swinging and puts his shirt back on. "That has no relevance regarding my current plan."

"You're not taking *their* reaction into account! The best and *only* defense we have is the bola. But I need that hideous devil far enough away from me to throw it. I'll hide while you talk to him. You've got to persuade him somehow to walk across the deck down to the stern!"

"Very well. I will engage White Wolf." He leans in close. "We know they shall react, but we cannot anticipate what that reaction will be. We shall be ready to pounce, to attack, to overpower and subjugate them, the way they did us. The African wild dog, the cinereous vulture and the bola will be instrumental in our assault. No more discussion. Come!" Tuk grabs the leash on the hook near Sleuth's cage. "Let us unbolt their cages and free the endangereds."

21
Was Ist Los?

I head to Mig's cage.

"*Free....*" Mig barks and leaps out with a picture of a rabbit running on the tundra.

Still retracted when I unlock her cage, I place Allia inside my pack, squeezed next to the scaly baby rolled in a ball. Antoadia slips into the mesh pocket on the outside.

Sleuth bursts out as soon as Tuk cracks his cage door. Buzzie flaps her massive wings three times, and sails through the open glass door.

Sending a picture—of her gliding above the yacht, I plead. "Don't go far!"

Squawking, she sends the same image back, "*Above I circle.*"

Sleuth leaps around the room, springing on the couches and tables. He's literally bouncing off the walls.

Tuk holds the leash, slapping his thigh. "Here boy, come here," and makes kissing noises, as if calling his pet poodle.

"Give it to me." I demand.

He tosses me the leash.

Sending a clear picture of the dog standing next to me, I point at my feet, "Sleuth, come! Now!" He jumps over the couch and stands next to me. Securing the leash to his collar, I send an image of the freak-a-droid next to the deformed devil. I follow this with another picture of Sleuth biting Big Bear's legs, and say, "We will find them. On my command, you attack the large machine man."

"The one with farcical feet," Tuk says, eyes bright.

Sleuth chirps an image of the freak-a-droid in pieces.

"He knows who I'm talking about."

"Let us go." Tuk heads toward the stairs.

"Wait." I scan the room. "Where'd Mig go? Did you see?" We both look around, but he's nowhere.

Tuk shakes his head. "I did not perceive where your little fox trotted off to."

"Mig, where are you?" I call, with a picture of me calling him on the tundra.

He sends a picture of a vole nest on the tundra. *"Hunting!"* Comes his cheerful reply.

I hesitate, then say, "We should go. He's off stalking somewhere."

"Very well," Tuk replies.

My knees are shaking hard. "One final thing, this is a surprise attack. We must be as quiet as possible."

"Of course," Tuk nods. "I shall be quiet as a mouse.... no.... not a mouse. Mice are noisy. I shall be quieter." His eyes light up. "As soundless as the anechoic chamber at Orfield Laboratories, in Minneapolis, Minnesota, the quietest place on earth, with a background noise reading of negative nine point four decibels. I shall be as quiet as absolute silence!"

Rolling my eyes, I whisper, "Great!"

"Considering the raucous nature of the species, did you ever consider that quiet as a mouse is a ridiculous expression?"

"Zip it!" I scowl.

He does.

Gripping the leash, I let Sleuth pull me up the stairs. I don't hear Tuk *at all* as we file through the door into the sunshine. The temperature on my cuff reads a blistering 122 degrees Fahrenheit. Limping past *Anniqsuqti's* stairs, I dig into my pocket and wrap my fingers around one of the stones, still cool. I will use it as soon as I have the chance. I've got make sure the creep is far enough away and standing free of any obstruction.

Even with Dad's thermoregulation Xip3 jacket, almost instantly my body feels sticky with tropical heat. A flock of storks flies overhead, landing on the shore near a bamboo forest where a shimmering golden pagoda rises, its stairs leading into the muddy river. Cargo barges, tourist boats, bamboo rafts, and immense log rafts float by in both directions. Nuwa's latest hit blares from a crowded ferryboat drifting past. The river narrows and more temples rise from distant green hills, their spires like drizzled sand. On the nearby riverbank, transport barges lie beached near small fishing out-riggers and rafts of floating bamboo.

Nuwa's voice fades as the ferryboat heads downriver. Holding my breath, I limp quietly toward the bridge and duck behind a column wide enough to hide us. Tuk is practically glued to my back. The freak-a-droid has his back to us and stands next to White Wolf, seated in the pilot's chair. Mandalay's harbor appears in the distance. The hideous man stands and scans the harbor with binoculars.

"Go in now, Tuk." I whisper over my shoulder. "You'll surprise them first. Get White Wolf out of there. Show him where you climbed up—or something, anything. Just get him to walk to the stern!"

I lean down to release the wild dog and stuff the leash in my pocket.

White Wolf mutters something and Big Bear turns. The ship slows and Tuk enters the bridge.

"Well... Mr. Tuttuk is a splendid swimmer." The devil rises with a smirk that melts into a sneer. "I hate liars!" he snarls. "Green Dragon is no *gang*! Green Dragon is only sushi! Too bad we arrive in Mandalay." He gestures toward the harbor. "My men wait for me there."

"On the contrary, it is too bad for you." Tuk replies with a smile. "We notified INTERPOL and WEAPP who await our arrival to arrest you and take control of the *Yanbu*."

When did he ever notify WEAPP or INTERPOL? He's bluffing, but I so wish it were true!

"You know nothing," White Wolf spits. "My Red Dragons are everywhere. I will never get arrested because they will never catch me! And how *did* you get back on board, anyway?"

"A sizable piece of flotsam conveniently wedged itself, which enabled me to make the climb." Tuk says.

"I do not believe you. The ship has sensors everywhere."

"Then you must see the tree for yourself." Tuk points. "Port side at the stern. It is likely lodged between sensors."

"I will indeed." White Wolf snarls and leaves the bridge.

I watch until he's at the very stern. "NOW, SLEUTH!" I shout and send a picture of the dog biting the freak-a-droid's feet.

His mouth opens wide, Sleuth leaps across the deck and heads straight for Big Bear's ankles. Instantly he rips off a foot.

The exposed wires, tubes and titanium spark, pop, and fizz as Sleuth tears into the other ankle.

"My appendages!" Big Bear bellows, falling face down with a thud at Tuk's feet. Quickly Tuk kneels to access the activation button at the base of the freak-a-droid's back. It's an awkward placement phased out with the XH5.

Reaching into my pocket I take a deep breath and unroll the bola.

Hearing the commotion, White Wolf turns. "Was ist los?" He yells, and hurriedly shuffles back.

This is my chance. Now. Heart pounds like a drum... exploding in my chest. Now. *NOW!* Adrenalin surges. I step away from the column and instantly everything slows down. I swing the bola hard, one full turn over my head, aim for his legs and release. It makes five revolutions as it whirls down the deck softly whipping the air. The stones almost shine in the sun flying across the white ship, and somehow it looks like my tattoo. It's a powerful strike. The stones smash into his ankles and circle his legs four times, binding them tightly together. A perfect throw.

White Wolf screams, "Big Bear! Zertrümmere seinen Kopf!" before collapsing in slow motion and grabbing his ankles.

The freak-a-droid rolls onto his back, grabs Tuk around the shoulders and in one explosive jerk, slams his head into Tuk's forehead. Tuk staggers backwards, his eyes roll up into his head and he collapses to the floor.

Coughing and gagging, Sleuth makes his way up Big Bear's legs ripping and crunching. The freak-a-droid squeaks louder, repeating, "My extremities! My extremities!"

White Wolf rolls onto his back clutching both ankles, moaning.

I'm trembling, vibrating head to foot. I did it...It's hard to believe...but *I really did it...* I need to get...to Tuk and Sleuth. The disgusting dragon writhes, rolling back and forth, wailing loudly. Did I break *both* of his ankles? I hope so! A ferry passes. Nuwa's song drifts louder....so familiar... probably one of Aanas' favorites. Buzzie circles overhead.

Focus. Focus mindsight. In a burst, I send Buzzie a picture—she's perched on the dragon's knees, "Need you NOW!"

She drops from the sky, swoops across the bow and lands. In three slow motion hops her talons clutch his knees.

I need to tie him up somehow, and approach slowly, scanning the deck for a piece of rope, then realize, I have the leash! I take it from my pocket and pull it taut between my hands. He's groaning so loudly that even with my limp, he's not aware of me. When I'm next to him, I see what my throw accomplished. One foot is oddly twisted at a right angle and both ankles are swelling. His eyes are closed, and his contorted face is grimacing with pain. His trembling hands rub his ankles. Kneeling, I wrap the leash around his legs and arms together, binding him good and tight. He'll never get loose with my favorite knot, the one Taata taught me—the Eskimo bowline.

"Ich bin ein dummkopf!" He yells, spitting as I untangle the bola from his ankles and stuff it in my pocket.

Limping across the deck to the bridge stairs, Sleuth appears. I point to White Wolf motionless, "Stay here," and send a picture of the dog sitting beside the wounded dragon.

He chirps a picture of Tuk in a heap on the floor surrounded by body parts. "*Your Machine man sleeps. The fat one, dead.*"

22
Neural Network Damage and a Werewolf?

Hopping down the stairs, I hold tight to the railing and limp to the bridge where Tuk slumps on the floor surrounded by Big Bear's electronic remains. His mauled remnants are exploded in pieces everywhere, except for his head, intact. The whirring, beeping, and clunking of dying drives fills the room. Sleuth ripped almost every piece of the freak-a-droid apart. Specks of blue oil fleck the bridge like a dot painting. The largest piece, his arm-less torso is punctured like a pin cushion. Teeth marks line each side of the freak-a-droid's torso oozing a steady stream of oil. It looks like he was assaulted by a pod of killer whales, not a lone wild dog.

Careful not to step on any parts, I limp to Tuk and kneel, laying him out flat on the floor. I feel around for the concave belly button and press. Nothing. I press again. Still nothing.

"Come on..." I whisper. Pushing the button again and holding as I count aloud, "One one thousand, two one thousand, three one thousand..." When I reach ten one thousand, his eyes flicker, his mouth opens, and the three tones blow in my face. I recite the numerical passcode quickly, "9, 1, 5, 2, 0, 3, 9."

He jumps to his feet and stomps.

"What happened?" he asks in a monotone, like a common automaton.

Something is *so* wrong, and wonder if I can fix him.

"Sleuth happened."

He stomps again. "Too bad." He jerks his head back and forth six, maybe seven times.

"Too bad? What's too bad?" I ask, not sure I want to hear the answer.

"I did not get to watch the painted dog's jaws rip that anus-of-an-android apart," he says, and pulls his lips back like he's looking at his teeth in a mirror. He's trying to smile, but his lips don't curl. The freak-a-droid *must* have damaged his neural network.

"Look!" I wave my arm. "We're on the road to Mandalay, about to dock. Did you contact WEAPP and INTERPOL, like you said?"

He shakes his head, "I did not say that," and stomps again. "Androids feel."

I want to shout, 'No, they *don't!* Droids never feel!' but tell myself to be calm, gentle. Speak softly. "That's what you said before the freak-a-droid gave you that massive head-butt. Remember?"

His eyes blink furiously. "I lied...how about that? I never knew how easy it was to say something false and deceitful." He squints and shoves my shoulder hard.

Losing my balance, I almost fall.

"Ha, ha, ha," he says in his disconnected, staccato. His speech no longer flows. "I am more human than you ever thought possible."

I feel sorry for him. He sounds like a *total* robot. I wish Korave were here. He'd know how to fix him. I lean in, peering at his forehead, searching for a crack, a tear in his smartskin.

He jerks his head back. "What happened to Red Wolf?"

"You mean White Wolf? I wounded him with my bola.... pretty sure I broke his ankles."

"You are a brilliant hominid, Luki Sloan." He nods.

Poor Tuk. I almost regret reactivating him.

Expressionless, as if staring through me, he says, "I did my utmost."

"You did. You *definitely* did." I nod.

He licks his lips. "Where is Red Wolf now?"

Clearing my throat, I stop myself before correcting him again. "I left him on the deck. I'll contact WEAPP and IN-TERPOL."

He starts licking his lips. "I am capable of making a lightscreen call and intend to perform the operation," he points to the communication console, adding, "Androids feel!"

I agree, not wanting to irritate him. "Androids *do* feel... and since my bionic foot's broken, after you make the call, please bring Sleuth and Buzzie back to our ship."

As Tuk tiptoes between Big Bear's body parts and oil puddles, the *Yanbu's* autopilot kicks into reverse. The engines rev, and the ship glides to a stop alongside a bamboo raft on the riverbank.

It doesn't matter that neither one of us knows how to activate the superyacht's gangway. Men in t-shirts and shorts carry planks of wood on their heads onto the *Yanbu* deck. Expertly they lay the planks and create a ramp leading down to the bamboo raft. Once the final plank is in place, a short, brown-skinned woman with a black bun wearing an azure WEAPP uniform rushes across. A group of female officers trails her in identical outfits and in seconds the deck is crawling with WEAPPs.

The officers don't look that much older than me, and I'm not surprised. Mom always said women made better WEAPP officers than men. She said that intuition, empathy, patience and compassion are more innate in women than men, and important qualities when working with animals.

Captain Bo, the first WEAPP officer to cross, listens to my story while we stand waiting for the EMT's in the blazing heat. Tuk stands beside me in a trance, staring at the battered dragon. I'm glad he lets me do the talking.

One officer takes photographs of White Wolf, *Anniqsuqti*, and the *Yanbu* deck. Two men in tan shorts and shirts arrive with a narrow stretcher. White Wolf moans loudly as they lift and strap him onto the stretcher.

"Before they take me," White Wolf groans, "can you remove my mask? I get you. My face burns up inside this silicone."

Mask? Why would he wear a mask on his own boat?

"You do not deserve my compassion, but I will honor your request." Captain Bo says, and walks over peering inches from his face. Carefully she digs her fingernails around his hairline and pulls slowly. It takes her several minutes of gentle picking and pulling. When she steps away, she holds a thin, rubbery mask revealing his face that's completely covered in hair!

"He's a real werewolf?!" I gasp. His face is the color of bright salmon because he's so hot, and his cheeks all the way up to his eyes, including his eyelids, nose, and forehead, are covered in thick, fuzzy, almost pure white hair! Instantly I feel sorry for him.

"Hypertrichosis," Tuk says with a stomp, "an extremely rare condition caused by additional genes in the X chromosomes. It is a genetic disease that runs in families."

"Because he is the last descendant of the Hapsburg dynasty," Captain Bo says.

"Hapsburg dynasty?" I ask, and realize I'd feel a lot sorrier for him if he weren't so wicked.

"A royal German family and one of the main European empires from the fifteenth to the twentieth century. Mating with family members over centuries caused the distinctive Hapsburg nose and enlarged lower jaw with the extended chin," Tuk says with a stomp.

"He looked that way because his family mated with each other?" I ask.

"Indeed. His facial deformities were the direct result of the family's inbreeding. And the reason he used countless masks to hide his abnormality, along with numerous aliases, which is how he evaded capture for many years. WEAP knew his identity, but he was quite devious using phony passports from dozens of countries, which is why we were unable to apprehend him for so long."

"So, who is he, really?" I ask.

"He is Austrian and his real name is Alfons Leopold von Otto." Captain Bo says.

"Take me to an air-conditioned ambulance before I die of heat stroke!" White Wolf groans.

Captain Bo waves the men to take him away.

Once he's gone, she turns back to me. "WEAPP now takes charge of your endangereds, and the pig. They will be returned to their home countries into reserves and preserves for protection."

"Thank you." I nod and feel the pangolin uncurling in the pack against my back. "Wait! I still have the baby!" I slip off the jacket and unzip the backpack.

Antoadia scrunched herself to the bottom of the mesh pouch, out of the sun. Allia opened in the heat. Passing the scaly baby to Captain Bo, I ask, "Is it okay if I say goodbye to the endangereds before you take them? I mean, after we find my pet fox?"

"Of course." She passes the pangolin and empty baby bottle to her lieutenant, who scurries down the gangway to a WEAPP Medi-truck. "We will take charge of the animals that the Green Dragons collected after you find your fox. Excuse me now." She turns and heads to the bridge.

"Here," I pass Allia and Antoadia to Tuk, "Take them back to our ship. I'll wait for you at the top of the stairs in the saloon. We've got to find Mig."

"I shall assist to locate your arctic fox." Tuk says and stomps off.

I feel like a rubbery, blubbery piece of muktuk. It doesn't help that Nuwa's song fills the hot, humid air, her voice screeching from every passing ferry. Jamming my fingers in my ears, I close my eyes, inhale and lick the salty skin above my lip. My tongue and throat are dry as dust. It's as if my entire body, every cell, craves water. Exhale. Inhale. Stomach growls. Come on... focus...inhale. Impossible. Too tired. Way too thirsty. Need air conditioning. Limping to the top of the stairs through the doors into the frigid air, I sit trying to focus my mindsight, trying to find my Mig... where are you Mig? In a flash... in my mindsight, he's *there*... in murky gloom.

"Mig! Where are you?" I ask with a picture of me calling him on the tundra.

A burst of images, of swooping stairs appears in my mindsight. *"Down, down, down. Into burning night,"* his voice purrs in my mind's ear.

Standing too fast, I slip and grab the railing. I'm falling, just as Tuk appears.

23
Down into the Dark

The first set of stairs leads to the bridge, where a petite WEAPP officer takes pictures of the freak-a-droid's parts from every angle. Captain Bo and three officers stare at lightscreens. They're engrossed in studying the ship's log—where it cruised and when, which ports it docked in and its cargo. Ignoring us, we keep going. To catch me if I fall, Tuk goes down backwards. Hopping carefully down each step, I grip the railing as we descend into a room filled with furniture.

I scan the room crowded with chairs and tables. Leopard skin pillows adorn cherry velvet couches beside overstuffed chairs in peacock blue. "Looks like some sort of club."

Tuk replies, "A club for criminals who traffic endangereds." He walks stiffly across zebra skins covering the floor towards a glossy black bar.

I'm lightheaded. The stripes all over the floor don't help. "I could use your shoulder."

Gazing at the mirrored shelves behind the bar stacked to the ceiling with liquor bottles, Tuk stomps his feet and turns, expressionless. "You were born with shoulders. Why do you require mine?"

"To lean on! I'm dizzy and my bionic foot is useless!"

"I am able to do that." He walks back and nudges his shoulder into my stomach.

"No… just stand next to me." I pull his arm. "Come on, be normal. I need your support to help me walk. Got it?"

He nods, "Got it." Staring at the ground, he adds, "Androids feel."

"I guess so, Tuk…you do feel." I lie and rub his arm. To repeat that phrase is such an odd glitch in his system, it almost seems like he's trying to convince me. Droids may *want* to feel, but there's no way they feel. All they do is *process*. That's it. That's all they *ever* do.

Gripping his arm, I cross the dizzying stripes, hop-limping to another set of stairs. We descend further into a dining room where a massive crystal chandelier hangs like a frozen waterfall above a long, rectangular table with chairs that sit shoulder to shoulder, like soldiers. An enormous golden throne stands at the head of the table. The monstrous chair shimmers with two thrashing dragons, their scales twinkling with gemstones.

"I want to touch the chair. Are you able to you stand a moment without my support?"

"Sure. I'll lean on the table. But why do you need to feel the chair exactly?"

"To determine the authenticity of the gems."

"With your fingers?"

He nods mechanically.

"Go ahead. I'm curious."

He walks to the chair and runs his hands over the dragons' glittering gems.

Abruptly, my mindsight flashes on White Wolf sitting on the velvet seat of his jewel-encrusted throne, resting his hands on dragon spine armrests. He's eating, drinking, laughing with Red Dragon captains from all parts of the world, together to celebrate their success selling endangereds. Shaking my head to release the vision, I shudder at the suffering they've caused.

"Eighteen karat gold dragons with grade A rubies, emeralds and diamonds from one to three carats," Tuk announces with a stomp.

"I'm not surprised. Let's keep going."

Gripping Tuk's arm, we descend lower into a bedroom with ebony walls. Daylight cracks at the edge of heavy curtains.

"Pull the curtains Tuk, so we can look around." I steady myself on a chair.

He opens the curtain wide. "We are at sea level, next to the dock. WEAPP has barricaded the waterfront."

I grope my way over and watch a procession of officers walk down the wooden gangway carrying mesh bags stuffed with pangolins. WEAPP ambulances and Medi-trucks line the street behind the blockade. Like a dragonfly at rest, further up the riverbank, a WEAPP helicopter waits for an emergency.

With a shiver, I realize that real tiger skins cover the floor. Leopard skins cover the huge bed, their heads resting on pillows, their massive canines gleaming, frozen in a growl.

The next stairway brings us to the kitchen. Pots and pans dangle from hooks overhead. In the way back, a Dutch door is open halfway.

Spying a square metal sink, I hop over and turn on the cold water faucet full blast, drenching my head, gulping. Water never tasted so good! I let it run down my neck and over my head until I'm satisfied. With my head soaking wet, I turn the water off and hop toward the Dutch door.

Bending over the bottom half of the door, I squint into the darkness. More stairs. Steep industrial metal steps, almost vertical. Even with crimson lights on the walls, it's as dim as

Wales at midnight in February. Tuk squeezes next to me for a look.

"This leads to the lowest level—the cargo and storage areas," Tuk tells me.

"Mig's down there." I reply and pull the bottom half open.

Metal railings hug each side of the narrow stairs. Like a gymnast on parallel bars, I grip the railings and let my upper body do the work, propelling me downward. Halfway down, I stop and listen to a soft buzzing that sounds like insects. There's an earthy pong in the air, like a rainforest, wet and green. Suddenly, something moves at the very bottom.

24

A Jungle? A Cryolab? Mom and Dad?

"Is that you, Mig?" I call down.

"*Hungry!*" he barks with a picture of... a monkey?

Crimson light drenches the hallway as I ease off the last step. Mig trots off with an excited squeal. Relieved, I follow, limping behind him and lean on Tuk's shoulder.

We're heading toward the stern when Mig makes a left into a hall up the starboard side. The buzzing grows louder. We haven't gone far when the hall opens into a cargo area the width of the ship. There, in the bloodshot darkness, behind a fine mesh screen that hangs from the ceiling to the floor is... a jungle!? It's a miniature forest with a tangle of vines, orchids, trees and ferns. And clinging to the trees and vines with the tiniest padded fingers and round, unblinking eyes are dozens of furry creatures the size of my fist—all staring at us. It's as if owls had mated with monkeys to create these magical beings. Some have tiny infants clinging to their backs. One catches a cricket and stuffs it in its mouth, crunching and smacking. I hop closer as quietly as I can. The buzzing grows louder, and all ears turn toward me. *They're* buzzing a soft, bird-like trill. Their chorus of contentment is a tranquil droning, like a purr. They're not at all stressed.

"They're incredible – *whatever* they are!" I whisper.

"Luzon Tarsiers, from the Philippines. The oldest, smallest known primate in the world," Tuk whispers.

A spasm of disgust hits me when I wonder what the disfigured demon had planned for them.

Tuk continues, "Tarsiers are exceptionally rare, sensitive, shy, nocturnal creatures. A stressed Tarsier can commit suicide by willing themselves to die."

"What?!" I gasp so loudly they all turn toward me.

"To die quickly," Tuk continues, "if you so much as hold one in your hands, it will be under such stress, it will stiffen and eventually stop breathing."

"That's too horrible for words!" I blurt and glance at Mig. He watches with only one thing in mind—whether tarsier tastes better than rabbit.

"Don't even think about it!" I murmur and flick my finger on his head.

He sends an image of Mom and Dad, turns with a yip and trots down the hall behind us. A cloud of butterflies fills my stomach. Really? Could it be? "Follow that fox," I say to Tuk.

Mig trots along the port side, up a hall behind the same stairs we'd come down. We come to a door, and Mig squeals with excitement, sending pictures of Mom at the sink and Dad at the kitchen counter cleaning salmon? What? Dad tosses Mig the tail.... "*Here*!" Mig declares.

I turn the door handle. It opens easily—into a freezing cold hall flooded with blinding bright light. Shielding my eyes, there's another door on the left. I turn the handle; it opens and I stick my head inside. The overhead light flashes on automatically. I scan the room filled with gleaming metal tanks. There's a table with two high-powered electron microscopes, a few lightscreen stations and a door in the middle of the wall that probably leads to a supply a closet. "It's just a lab," I mutter.

Tuk steps stiffly inside and looks around. "This laboratory contains equipment for one thing exclusively...."

"Yeah?" My eyebrows go up.

"Cryopreservation."

Every other tank has a nitrogen label with a flexible metal hose that leads from the nitrogen lid to squat, shiny tanks alongside them. Each smaller tank has a digital keypad and small screen.

"Dad does cryopreservation at our home lab."

"With nitrogen gas cooled to minus 196 Celsius, these tanks have the capacity for organelles, cell tissues and extracellular matrix of thousands of creatures.... no...let me correct myself...make that...." He pauses and counts. "Ten tanks, each one containing twenty-five hundred vials...."

My jaw drops. "That's twenty-five thousand endangereds?!"

Tuk approaches the nearest tank, pops the latch, and lifts the lid on hinges. Frozen nitrogen pours out and cascades over the edge, like milky smoke. Bending his face over the tank, he blows to clear the vapor. He dips his hand inside, lifts a vial out and tilts his head to read the label. "Black rhinoceros," he utters, puts it back and pulls another, "Javan rhinoceros," and another, "Orangutan," and another, "Sumatran elephant," and another, "Western lowland gorilla."

"All endangereds!" I gasp.

"Critically," he nods mechanically.

Mig squeals and sends a picture of Mom in the kitchen holding a jar of peanut butter with Mig on his hind legs licking her finger.

"Come on." Limping into the hall, I try the next door. Locked. There's a keypad of numbers and letters on the wall. I hear muffled voices inside.

"Mom? Dad? Is that *you*?!" I shout through the door crack and listen. I can't make out what they're saying—if it is them, and turn to Tuk who's staring blankly at the keypad.

"It could be a billion trillion different combinations." I sigh, my shoulders dropping.

"Or something simple, something obvious, something we already know." He stomps. "Something about the *Yanbu*, perhaps?"

"How about the name, White Wolf?"

"White Wolf is 944839653." He rattles off the numbers.

"Maybe." I shrug, spelling out White Wolf on the pad, and try the handle. Still locked.

"Perhaps it is 2442327? That is Big Bear." He watches over my shoulder.

I input Big Bear and try the handle again. Still locked. "I'll try Red Dragon. Repeat those numbers, please."

"733372466."

I enter the numbers; the keypad turns green. I try the handle and it *turns*!

Mom and Dad sit on a couch and stare in wide eyed disbelief.

"Mom! Dad!" I rush toward them but can't get close. They're behind a gate with thin, pale bars from the floor to the ceiling.

"Luki??!" they shout, jumping off the couch.

"What are *you* doing here?!" Dad roars, shaking his head. "I can't believe it!"

I exclaim, "Neither can I!"

"How did you get here?!" Mom cries.

"The wall has a keypad on it, there." Dad points, "... Just out of our reach."

"Enter 92628!" Mom blurts. "I memorized it the one time that idiot droid came in to unlock the lab door from our side."

"92628 spells Yanbu." Tuk stomps, licking his lips.

Entering the numbers, the keypad turns green, the door releases, and I run, jumping into Dad's arms. He squeezes me so tight I can hardly breathe, but I don't want him to stop, *ever*. Mom hugs me from behind. Mig jumps and yips at our feet.

25
Endangered DNA and the Last Pangolins

Tuk watches us hug and stomps once. "Hello, Frank and Virginia. It is good to perceive you. Androids feel."

"Tuttuk!" Dad sticks his hand out to shake and keeps one arm tightly wrapped around my shoulder. Mom has her arm snug around my waist. They're wearing identical silk pajamas, but Dad's are way too small and barely come below his calves, and his sleeves end just below his elbows. Moms' are way too big. The pants pool around her feet and the sleeves swallow her hands.

Tuk takes Dad's hand and pumps it.

"You okay, Tuttuk?" Dad glances at me with a frown.

I answer before Tuk has a chance to. "That freak-a-droid head-butted him hard. He hasn't been the same since I reactivated him."

Dad nods. "Neural network damage... if we're lucky it's just a component or two. Eh, Tuttuk?" He moves closer, looking into Tuk's eyes.

"Yes, Frank. That would be.... lucky..." Tuk agrees, "... Luki has damage too. If she is lucky, her ankle will require a single screw."

"What happened to your foot?" Dad pouts.

"I broke it kicking my way out of White Wolf's cage."

"And why is your hair soaking wet?" Mom asks.

"We'll tell you about it on the trip home. Okay, Tuk?" I smile, hoping he might smile back, but he can't.

Tuk nods, "I would like that."

"What are we waiting for?" Dad says. "Let's get out of here!"

"It's a long climb." I warn.

Tuk adds, "Five stories."

"You're not climbing anywhere except piggyback." Dad turns, squats and sticks his arms out.

Wrapping my arms his neck, he lifts me on his back.

Mig leads the way up toward the light.

"With so many Blue Trance Micro Bolts, we were unconscious in seconds." Mom says.

Out of breath from carrying me, Dad adds, "We were out cold at least forty-eight hours. When we came to, we were caged in that room and had no idea where we were." He catches his breath, looks around and out the saloon window. "Glad our WEAPPs are out there."

"Am I correct that they kidnapped you because White Wolf's chief scientist was killed in an accident?" Tuk asks.

"Or murdered... they still don't know," Mom adds.

"They never found his body," Dad says and stops to look at the wall of cages.

"But you're right, Tuttuk," Mom says. "White Wolf kidnapped us because of our experience, chiefly Frank's expertise with CRISPR and gene editing."

I don't understand. "But why?"

Mechanically Tuk asks, "What were his plans for the genetic material in his collection? De-extinction could not have been his goal. Was it Frank?"

I'm confused. "He didn't want to create more endangereds, did he? That doesn't make any sense."

Mom's eyes scrunch. "That evil man wanted to corner the market on endangered DNA."

Dad eases me off his back and on to the white couch where I'd sat next to that hideous, evil man. I get goosebumps.

"I thought he only cared about making tons of money from selling endangereds." I say.

"He saw it as the future of his business." Mom says.

"Of course!" Tuk bursts. "It is not many years before all these endangereds are extinct."

"Precisely," Dad nods, "at which point White Wolf would possess nearly all the endangered DNA in the world and could command *any* price."

"He's diabolical," Mom says with a shudder, "selling to the most unscrupulous scientists."

"He was not interested in de-extinction, Tuttuk," Dad says with a shake of his head. "He had zero interest in bringing endangereds back to life."

"He wanted Dad to replicate endangered DNA for the *money*...it was all about the *MONEY!*" Mom exclaims with disgust. "What do you say we step out on deck and get a little of that fresh, tropical air."

"It's been a while," Dad says.

Captain Bo is waiting for us when we reenter the saloon.

"I am honored to meet the doctors Sloan," she says with prayerful hands and a bow.

"How did you know?" I ask.

"In addition to the time, date, weather, course alterations and ports, Big Bear added the names of your parents to the ships' log, as if they were passengers." She chuckles, shaking her head.

"What an idiot," Mom snickers.

"We found Luzon Tarsiers in the cargo area of the bow," Tuk reports.

"Big Bear noted them in the log as well," Captain Bo nods. "They will remain where they are, and as soon as we have completed our investigation, they will be taken to Bohol Island on the *Yanbu*."

"Shouldn't they go back as soon as possible?" I ask.

She shakes her head. "Oh no. To maintain optimum health, security and tranquility of the shy, delicate primates... indeed...in order to ensure their survival.... we must, for the time being, do absolutely nothing."

Dad swivels his head toward me, and out of the corner of his mouth asks, "Tarsiers?"

"Mig found them. Isn't that right, boy?"

Mig looks up at me and sends a picture of voles in his bowl.

"He's hungry... and... I'd like to say goodbye to the endangereds."

"WEAPP ensures the endangereds will be homed in protected habitats and reserves," Captain Bo says.

"What about the Mangalitsa?" Tuk asks.

"Any creature that escapes the slaughterhouse deserves to live free and happy on a sanctuary farm," Captain Bo replies.

"Yes, indeed," Dad chuckles, "and your mother and I will be happy, once we're free of these pajamas!"

"You should be immensely proud of your daughter," Captain Bo says. "This is the largest shipment of Pangolins ever intercepted... and indeed, the last individuals of this species in the world."

"I did? I mean, we did?!"

"Our faunal transport helicopters will return them to the Philippines and release them into WEAPP-protected forests with 24-hour drone surveillance and armed patrols to guard them."

"Wow.... that's incredible," I say.

Captain Bo nods again with prayerful hands. "Thank you, Luki Sloan. WEAPP and INTERPOL owe you and your android an enormous debt of gratitude for your bravery and your selfless act of service. You saved 1,357 Pangolins."

"Incredible!" Dad exclaims.

"However, this does not include the tens of thousands of endangereds you saved that White Wolf intended to smuggle *in the future*. INTERPOL and the Asian WEAPP divisions commend and thank you for your team's extraordinary effort," she says, bowing deeply.

A ferryboat passes, blasting Nuwa again... the same song I've heard pieces of all day, and suddenly realize the song isn't Aana's favorite—it's *my* song! But how did Tuk do it?!

26
Flying Backwards in Time

Captain Bo didn't care that opening *Anniqsuqti's* cargo ramp damaged the *Yanbu* landing pad for Hogman's release. When I asked how they were going to get him off the boat, she said they would have to use a crane.

Once Hogman was off *Anniqsuqti*, my parents showered, got into their own clothes, and Tuk made a replacement screw for my foot with the 3-D printer while I spent the last grateful moments alone with Allia, Sleuth, Buzzie, Antoadia and the Slimediggers.

We're at 65,000 feet on cruise control for the seven-hour flight home. Dad and I sit at the galley table across from Mom. We're eating the last of the strawberries and Tuk's in the hall staring at us blankly.

"I didn't know I could care so much for a *reptile*," I say. "I think I'm going to miss Allia the most. She's so beautiful and thanks to her, I was able to hide the miniQ."

Mom cups my chin. "Oh sweetie, summer is right around the corner and it's your favorite time of year on the tundra.

You love foraging for roots and berries with Aana, fishing with Taata, and exploring with Mig." She pauses, pushing the hair from my eyes. "Plus, I'm counting on you and Tuttuk to help us count polar bears and their cubs in the preserve."

"I'm there!" I say cheerfully.

"Imagine….no Red Dragons in the strait this summer, thanks to you and Tuttuk!" Dad wraps his arm around my shoulders. "Your mother and I couldn't be prouder," he says, kissing the top of my head.

"And *you'll* have lots of time to spend in your favorite two places—the lab and the farmoire," I add with a grin.

"And work on thawing techniques after cryo preservation," Mom says. "Dad's on the verge of a breakthrough… we might well reverse the extinction soon."

"If we succeed, we'll help animals *and* plants!" Dad says and pops a berry in his mouth.

"We might even reverse damaged and threatened ecosystems. There may be environmental benefits with de-extinction," Mom adds.

Tuk stomps. "Unforeseen consequences not anticipated might occur with de-extinction."

Mom nods. "Yes, but…"

Tuk cuts her off with two stomps. "De-extinction may cause additional species to go extinct, create novel diseases, and force animals to live in captivity. De-extinction may not be beneficial to environments."

"That is correct, Tuttuk." Mom frowns and reaches for a berry.

"Plus, we've got to preserve habitats and restore ecosystems," I chip in.

"We're on the verge, but first we must reverse the big boil once and for all!" Dad exclaims with a fist.

Tuk frowns. "You make climate change sound like an infection."

"It is a sort of infection, isn't it, Tuttuk?" Mom asks.

"I did not consider that," he stomps, adding, "androids feel."

"It has taken decades, but slowly we are getting the big boil under control," Dad says, then changes the subject. "Hey, I think we ought to invite Korave for a visit. If he's such a wiz with droids, he can help diagnose Tuttuk. Heck, Korave can teach *me* a thing or two!"

"Korave is nice.... I like Korave." Tuk says flatly.

"This weekend?" Mom smiles.

My eyes brighten. "Before spring break is over? Really? You sure? Yes!" I grin. "I'll call him right now!"

"Not so fast," Mom raises her hands. "First we need to call Aana and Taata. They must be worried sick about you... I cannot believe Aana let you two go off to catch that wicked man and his idiot droid."

My heart sinks. Aana will never forgive me. I turn to Tuk and change the subject. "I'm dying to hear how you got my song to Nuwa!"

Mom gasps, "He did?!"

"Nuwa has experimental neuromorphic chips engineered with a logarithm that determines the songs the public will love. These are the only songs she sings. After we succeeded in hacking Big Bear, I hacked Nuwa and uploaded your song. The logarithm decided she had to sing it." Tuk tries to smile and bares his teeth like at the dentist.

"I knew she was a gynoid!" I cry.

"Amazing, Tuttuk," Dad says.

I'm smiling so hard my face hurts. "Thanks a ton, Tuk!"

"We certainly have a lot to celebrate!" Mom flashes her beauty queen smile. "Tuttuk, what time is it at home?"

"At this moment, it is eleven thirty, last night." Tuk replies.

"That's so weird. Really?" I ask.

He nods. "We fly against the earth's rotation, backwards in time."

"True." Dad nods.

"Tootega, call Aana. She's such a night owl, she's got to awake," Mom says.

My mouth goes dry as Aana's face appears in the lightscreen.

Sitting on the couch in her living room, Aana puffs her pipe. Taata sleeps beside her, his chin on his chest. Seeing Mom and Dad, she grabs the pipe from her mouth and cries out, "Virginia! Frank! Alive!... *in Russia*??!"

"I lied..." I sputter. "We never went to visit Korave... um.... Tuk and I took the AEV to find White Wolf."

Mom turns from the lightscreen. "You lied to Aana and Taata?"

My mouth droops. "I'm sorry, Aana, but I had to! I couldn't tell you the truth! You'd never let us go, and I didn't want you to worry!"

"She saved us!" Dad blurts, squeezing my shoulder. "And they saved the last pangolins from certain death!"

Aana turns to Taata and shakes him awake. "Taata, look! Frank and Virginia, ALIVE!"

"Mig was really the one who found Mom and Dad," I say.

Taata rubs his eyes and wags his finger. "One clever little arctic fox you got, Luki!"

"Luki caught White Wolf, too," Tuk adds, expressionless.

"LUKI?!" Aana and Taata exclaim in unison.

"Those Inupiaq skills come in mighty handy, huh?" Taata grins.

I nod, smiling hard. "Definitely!"

"Your lie does not matter," Aana shakes her head. "The outcome is magnificent and there is no pain from your falsehood."

"Extraordinary!" Taata shouts.

"You are one smart, lucky, *extraordinary* girl," Aana points, "we will celebrate this weekend…"

"With everyone in the village!" Taata smiles.

Aana clasps her hands to her chest. "Coming home now?"

"Touchdown is in six hours and forty-three minutes," Tuk reports.

"Time enough to sleep…" Taata snorts. "See you in the morning!"

"I'll make doughnuts!" Aana nods, smiling so hard her cheeks puff and her eyes disappear into slits.

"Plenty of time for me and Mom to hear how you and Tuttuk pulled this off," Dad smiles slyly.

Aana says, "And speaking of hearing, Nuwa has a new song you will love Luki, I am sure of it!"

"Yeah, I think I might like it… a lot," I say with a wide smile.

27
IMAGINE

Imagine no extinction
It's easy if you try
No climate change without them
No need to say goodbye
Imagine all the creatures
Content alive today
Imagine healthy oceans
It isn't hard to do
No plastic trash to choke them
No over fishing too
Imagine all the creatures
Living life in peace
You may say I'm a dreamer
But I'm not the only one
I hope today you'll join me
So we can all live as one
Imagine no pointless killing

Can you see it in your mind
No need for greed or hunger
Brothers and sisters of every kind
Imagine all the creatures
Sharing all the world
You may say I'm a dreamer
But I'm not the only one
I hope today you'll join me
So we can all live as one.

Original lyrics by John Lennon, 1971

28
DISCUSSION QUESTIONS

1. Luki's dad calls climate change the Big Boil. What other nicknames for climate change can you think of?

2. Luki says that humans haven't stopped climate change because of greed and stupidity. If you ruled the world, how would you encourage people to change their behaviors to help reverse climate change?

3. Why is it a bad idea to introduce non-native species into an ecosystem, like Luki does with the gigantic African wild dog in the VR adventure game with Korave?

4. Name a few characteristics of an invasive species that help it outcompete with native species causing it to disrupt the ecological balance.

5. Provide an example of how Luki's mindsight helps her.

6. One of the ways that Luki's family adapts to living in a cold climate is by growing vegetables in the farmoire. Give an example of an invention that would benefit people living in a very warm climate.

7. A circle with a dot inside is Aana's symbol for the Generative Principle. What symbol would you use to show that you care about your environment, and what action would you take to protect it?

8. What do White Wolf and the Red Dragons care most about?

9. How would you use clairvoyance if you could communicate with animals this way?

10. How would you feel if you had to lie in order to save the life of your parents or guardians? In what other circumstances would lying be justified?

11. If your vehicle had a Quantum Stealth Cloak that you could activate to help someone in trouble (or do a good deed), what or who would you use it for?

12. What caused the Partula snails to become endangered?

13. Puerto Rican crested toads are prey to mongoose and feral cats. What else caused their population decline?

14. African wild dogs are pack animals. What advantage does hunting in groups give predators?

15. What are the primary causes of the sixth mass extinction?

16. What are pangolin scales thought to be good for? How would you set up an experiment to test the validity of the scales' special property?

17. What is the petrochemical plague omnipresent on earth that Tuk refers to?

18. What does Taata mean by, "You got to row with your own oars. Nobody else's?" In what ways are your natural talents unique?

19. Tuk lists specific characteristics of endangered animals to White Wolf based on the short-term gain of their use as food, medicine and furniture. What argument could you make for keeping the animals alive on a long-term basis?

20. Why do women make better WEAPP officers than men, according to Luki's Mom?

21. Why does Tuk think that de-extinction may not be beneficial to the environment? Do you agree?

22. Overcoming her fears, Luki is courageous to fly off with Tuk and find White Wolf in the hopes of finding her parents. Do you believe courage is a natural trait for humans, or does courage arise out of necessity?

23. What happens to Tuk to damage his affective computing and what are his symptoms?

24. Luki lives in a world surrounded by technology but captures White Wolf with a simple, indigenous hunting tool. Do you believe technology is able to solve most of society's problems, or do you think we ignore simple solutions while relying on technology?

Afterword

The rate of **species extinction** is up to 10,000 times higher than the natural, historical rate. More than one in four species faces extinction, and unless urgent action is taken, the rate will rise to 50% by 2100. https://www.theworldcounts.com/challenges/planet-earth/forests-and-deserts/species-extinction-rate

30 x 30 is a worldwide initiative to address climate change and the loss of nature. The goal is to protect 30% of the world's lands and waters by 2030 to maintain biodiversity and defend against the climate crisis. https://www.wilderness.org/key-issues/30-x-30-movement

https://www.nrdc.org/resources/30x30-nrdcs-commitment-protect-nature-and-life-earth

Pangolins are one of the most trafficked mammals in Asia and Africa. All eight species of pangolin have been hunted for their meat, organs, skin and scales. Other body parts are valued for their use in traditional medicine. The IUCN classifies four species as vulnerable, two species as endangered and two species as critically endangered. https://www.worldwildlife.org/species/pangolin

https://www.iucnredlist.org/search?query=pangolin&searchType=species

The **African Wild Dog** is classified as one of the world's most endangered mammals. Threats include accidental and targeted killings by humans, rabies, distemper, habitat loss and competition by larger predators like lions. It is classified as endangered by the IUCN. https://www.worldwildlife.org/species/african-wild-dog

https://www.iucnredlist.org/species/12436/166502262

Declining since the 1800's, the **Cinereous Vulture** is the largest European vulture and one of the largest raptors in the world. It faced a dramatic decline in Europe, but is making a comeback from Portugal to France and Bulgaria thanks to an increase of the Spanish population. It is listed as near threatened by the IUCN. https://4vultures.org/vultures/cinereous-vulture/

https://www.iucnredlist.org/species/22695231/154915043

Partula snails, also known as the Polynesian tree snail or niho tree snail is in danger of extinction. This species was once common in Tahiti, but the IUCN now considers it extinct in the wild since the snail is primarily found in captivity. Efforts to reintroduce the snail to its native range are underway. https://www.nationalgeographic.com/animals/invertebrates/facts/partula-snail

https://www.zsl.org/what-we-do/projects/partula-snail-conservation

https://www.iucnredlist.org/species/103135035/103137318

Native to and most abundant in southern Madagascar is the **Radiated tortoise**, which has been introduced to the islands of Réunion and Mauritius. It is a very long-lived species, with recorded lifespans of up to 188 years. The IUCN classifies these tortoises as critically endangered due to habitat destruction and poaching. https://nationalzoo.si.edu/animals/radiated-tortoise

https://www.iucnredlist.org/species/9014/12950491

The **Puerto Rican crested toad** is the only toad species native to Puerto Rico. Threats to the toad's survival include habitat competition from invasive cane toads, which also eat crested toad tadpoles and toadlets. The crested toad's long list of predators includes cats, crabs, dogs, heron, lizards, mongooses, and rats. Agriculture and urban development, which destroys the toad's breeding pools has led to its decline as well. Other threats stem from natural disasters like hurricanes and drought, which damage vital habitats and prevent mating gatherings. The IUCN classifies it as endangered. https://www.nationalgeographic.com/animals/amphibians/facts/puerto-rican-crested-toad

https://www.iucnredlist.org/species/54345/172692429

Endemic to the Philippines is the **Luzon tarsier, or Philippine tarsier**, the world's second smallest primate. Known as the "world's smallest monkey," they are among the oldest land species that have existed continuously in the Philippines for the last 45 million years. These tarsiers have the largest eye-to-body ratio of all mammals. In relation to their bodies, their eyes are 150 times larger than a human's. Their heads can rotate as much as 180 degrees, and they can leap backward with precision. It is classified as near threatened according to the IUCN. https://animalia.bio/philippine-tarsier?endemic=14

https://www.iucnredlist.org/species/21492/17978520

The **Inupiat or Inupiaq** are a group of indigenous Alaskans whose traditional territory spans northeast from Norton Sound on the Bering Sea to the Canada – US border. Like all indigenous Arctic people, they are on the front line of climate change.
https://learninglab.si.edu/collections/the-i%C3%B1upiaq-people-and-their-culture/Ui4zV4tEG1Cn3BW2
https://www.nationalgeographic.com/environment/article/little-diomede-alaska-faces-rapid-climate-change-threatens-native-inupiat-community
https://www.atlasobscura.com/articles/climate-change-inupiat-northern-alaska

About Author

I was born in Liberia, Africa because my father was a diplomat. I was an infant when we moved to the U.S., but when I was five, we moved to Holland, which felt like being dropped on an alien planet. I went to a Dutch school where I learned to read, write and speak Dutch. My sister and I became fluent in a matter of months. I didn't learn to read or write English until I was eight. The first book I could read on my own was Dr. Seuss', *The Cat in The Hat*, which I loved. I have always loved animals too.

I am curious by nature and have done many different things for a living, including shucking scallops, waiting on tables, managing offices, producing TV commercials, writing internal communications for a multinational corporation, and much, much more. I am married and live with the sweetest rescue dog, three cats, four ducks and thousands of honeybees in New York's Hudson Valley. *EXTINCTION WARRIOR* is my first novel. I would love to hear what you think about it! http://www.susanbwile.com

Acknowledgments

Infinite, heartfelt gratitude goes to my partner, Carine Elen for her steadfast support and without whom Extinction Warrior would likely not exist.

Huge, heartfelt thanks goes to author, Kate Klimo for freely sharing her expertise, advice and wisdom along with her generous, no-holds-barred edit, which propelled me to the finish line and without whom this tale may have bored even the most avid reader.

Heartfelt thanks to Betty Marton for her copy editing and for bringing clarity and help to a variety of issues in the final stretch.

Heartfelt thanks to science educator, Cathy Law for the time she took to read not one, but two versions and for contributing discussion questions.

Thanks to Erin Young, developmental editor who helped me see where the story wanted to go.

With a promise that I will never again torture her (or anyone else) with a first draft, I'm grateful to Mary Lasby for reading what wasn't fit for consumption.

Thanks to Ceci Harris, Lexi and Dylan Friedman, my beta readers whose feedback improved the story.

A final note of thanks goes to my high school English teacher, Prudence Churchill, who set me on this path long ago.